D1084348

Of Course You Know That **Chocolate** Is a Vegetable

and Other Stories

Of Course You Know That **Chocolate** Is a Vegetable

and Other Stories

Barbara D'Amato

Five Star
Unity, Maine

Five Star First Edition Mystery Series
Published in 2000 in conjunction with
Tekno-Books and Ed Gorman.

Cover photograph by Smith & Powers.

Set in 11 pt. Plantin by Al Chase.

Printed in the United States on permanent paper.

Library of Congress Cataloging-in-Publication Data

D'Amato, Barbara
    Of course you know that chocolate is a vegetable and
other stories / by Barbara D'Amato. — 1st ed.
        p.   cm. — (Five Star standard print mystery)
    Contents: Dolley Madison and the staff of life — I vant to
be alone — Hard feelings — The lower Wacker Hilton —
Shelved — Soon to be a minor motion picture — If you've
got the money, honey, I've got the crime — Stop thief! —
See no evil — Freedom of the press — Of course you know
that chocolate is a vegetable — Motel 66.
    ISBN 0-7862-2539-4 (hc : alk. paper)
    1. Detective and mystery stories, American. I. Title.
II. Five Star standard print mystery series.
PS3554.A4674 O42   2000
813′.54—dc21   00-024236

TABLE OF CONTENTS

Of Course You Know That Chocolate Is a Vegetable   7

Dolley Madison and the Staff of Life   21

I Vant to Be Alone   27

Hard Feelings   36

The Lower Wacker Hilton   51

Shelved   69

Soon to Be a Minor Motion Picture   81

If You've Got the Money, Honey, I've Got the Crime   99

Stop, Thief!   118

See No Evil   131

Freedom of the Press   154

Motel 66   162

INTRODUCTION

I love mysteries. One day many, many years ago, I had been home sick, feeling horrible, and generally also feeling sorry for myself. My husband bought *Murder on the Orient Express* and said, "Read this. Enjoy." For the two or three hours I was reading it, I didn't notice that I felt sick. I was hooked. For many years, I read about three hundred mysteries a year. It seemed to me that a normal day was (1) work, (2) make dinner, (3) read a mystery. Lately, in an effort to get some writing done, I've cut back to maybe half a mystery a day.

When my son Paul was a little boy, he occasionally suffered from asthma. We were far away from civilization one night when he had an attack, and we were able to control it by giving him coffee while we drove over winding roads to the nearest hospital. By the way, despite the story, chocolate really is a vegetable and is actually good for you.

Of Course You Know that Chocolate

Is a Vegetable

"Of course you know that chocolate is a vegetable," I said.

"Lovely! That means I can eat all I want," Ivor Sutcliffe burbled, reaching his fork toward the flourless double-fudge cake.

Eat *more* than you want, you great tub of guts, I thought. The tub-of-guts part was rather unfair of me; I could stand to lose a pound or two myself. What I said aloud was, "Of course it's a vegetable. Has to be. It's not animal or mineral, surely. It grows on a tree—a large bush, actually, I suppose. It's as much a vegetable as pecans or tomatoes. And aren't we told to have several servings of vegetables every day?"

We were seated at a round table covered with a crisp white cloth at Just Desserts, a scrumptious eatery in central Manhattan that specializes in chocolate desserts, handmade chocolate candy, and excellent coffees. Just Desserts was willing to serve salads and a few select entrees to keep themselves honest, but if you could eat chocolate, why would you order anything else?

"I must say, Ms. Grenfield, it's very handsome of you to invite me after my review of your last book," Ivor said, dropping a capsule on his tongue, which then took the medication inside, his mouth closing like a file drawer. He washed down the medication with coffee.

I said, "No hard feelings. Reviewing books is your job."

"I may have been just a bit harsh."

Harsh? Like scrubbing your eyeball with a wire brush is harsh? I said, "Well, of course an author's feelings get hurt for a day or two. But we can't hold it against the critic. Not only is it his job, but, to be frank, it's in our best interests as writers to keep on pleasant terms. There are always future reviews to come, aren't there?"

"Very true."

Ivor's review had begun:

In *Snuffed*, the victim, Rufus Crown, is dispatched with a gaseous fire extinguisher designed for use on fires in rooms with computer equipment and other such unpleasant hardware, though neither the reader nor the fictional detectives know this at the start when his dead, but mysteriously unblemished body is found. The reader is treated to long efforts—quite incompatible with character development—on the part of the lab and medical examiner to establish what killed him.

"That's right, give away the ending," I had snarled to myself when I read this.

Snuffed had been universally praised by the critics and I thought I was a shoo-in for an award until the Ivor Sutcliffe review came out.

At the awards banquet, where I was not a nominee, fortune had seated me next to Sutcliffe. Just when the sorbet arrived, and I had happily pictured him, facedown, drowning in strawberry goo, he began to wheeze. My mind had quickly changed to picturing him suffocating. But he had popped a capsule in his greedy pink mouth and after a few minutes he quit wheezing.

Since one has to be moderately cordial at these events, or at least appear to be, I asked courteously, "Do you have a cold?"

"Asthma," he said.

"Sorry to hear that. My son had asthma. Seems to have outgrown it."

"Lucky for him. What did he take for it?"

I said, "Theophylline."

"Ah, yes. That's what my doctor gave me. So proud of his big words, just like you. Standard treatment, I believe. I have been taking it for several weeks." He said it as if conferring a great benediction upon the drug.

I was about to relate an incident about the time my husband, son, and I were on a camping trip, without the theophylline. We'd left it at home, since it had been many months since Teddy's last attack, and we weren't expecting trouble. Then Teddy had developed a wheeze. As evening came on, it got worse. And worse. There's nothing scarier than hearing your child struggle for breath. We were two hours away from civilization, and my husband and I panicked. We packed Teddy into the car, ready to race to the nearest country hospital; then I had called Teddy's doctor on my cell phone.

"Do you have any coffee?" he said. Well, of course we had. Who went camping without coffee?

"Give him some. Caffeine is chemically similar to theophylline. Then drive to the hospital."

All this I was about to tell Sutcliffe when something stopped me. It was not more than the faint aroma of an idea, a distant stirring of excitement. So—theophylline and caffeine were similar. Hmm.

Teddy had been warned to take his theophylline as directed, but never to overdose.

9

Then and there I invited Sutcliffe out to a "good will" snack the following week. He accepted. Well, *my* will was going to feel the better for it.

Sutcliffe's review had gone on:

> I deplore the substitution of technical detail for real plotting. One could amplify the question "Who Cares Who Killed Roger Ackroyd?" by asking, "Who cares how Roger Ackroyd was killed?" No one cares what crime labs and pathologists really do.

"Agatha Christie cared," I had whispered as I read it, trying not to gnash my teeth. "And Dorothy Sayers and just about everybody then—and just about everybody now on any bestseller list—Crichton, Clark, Cornwell, Grisham." In the first place, readers like to learn things. Second, technology is real and it's *now*. Third, it's exacting. Keeps a writer honest. You can't fake technical detail; it has to be right. You can't use the untraceable exotic poison these days. It has to be something people know about or even use every day. Or know they *should* know about. Then it's tantalizing.

But Ivor Sutcliffe wasn't scientific-minded. A know-it-all who knew nothing. A gross, hideous, undisciplined individual with bad table manners. I had once seen him, at a banquet, eat his own dinner and the dinners of three other guests who had failed to show.

So after the banquet I went home to my shelf of reference books, looking for something I almost knew about, or knew I should know about—just like a reader of fiction. I keep a large shelf of reference books. Having them to hand saves time, effort, and parking fees.

What would an overdose of theophylline do to a human being?

I turned first to the *Physician's Desk Reference*. This is a huge volume, 2,800 pages of medications, with their manufacturers, their brand names, their appearance shown in color pictures, their uses, their dosages, their effects, their adverse effects, and—overdosage.

An overdosage of theophylline was serious business. It said, "Contact a poison control center." That was good. One didn't issue that kind of warning for minor side effects. I read on. One had to monitor the dose carefully. Apparently the useful dose and dangerous dose were not far apart. I read on. Overdosage could produce restlessness, circulatory failure, convulsion, collapse, and coma. Or death.

Theophylline in normal use, it said, relaxed the smooth muscles of the bronchial airways and pulmonary blood vessels, acting as a bronchodilator and smooth-muscle relaxant. That was why it helped an asthma attack.

And then the punch line: "Theophylline should not be administered concurrently with other xanthines." And what were xanthines?

I turned to my unabridged dictionary. Why, xanthines included theophylline, caffeine (given Teddy's experience, this was no surprise) and the active ingredient of chocolate, theobromine. Aha!

Hmm. Being similar, they would have an additive effect, wouldn't they? Synergistic maybe? I turned to the *Merck Manual*, also huge, a 2,700-page volume, a bible of illnesses, their causes and treatments. In its section on poisons, caffeine poisoning was in the same sentence with theophylline poisoning. Among the symptoms of both were restlessness, circulatory-system collapse, and convulsions.

A medical text told me that fifty percent of theophylline convulsions result in death.

Isn't this fun? Research is so rewarding.

Well, I knew that theophylline was potentially deadly. Now what about the caffeine?

My book on coffees from around the world told me that a cup of coffee, depending on how strong it's brewed, contains 70 to 150 milligrams of caffeine. Drip coffee is strongest. Well, what about the extra-thick specialty coffees at Just Desserts? Could I assume they might have 200 milligrams?

What the book didn't tell me was how much caffeine would kill.

I pulled out the *Merck Index*, a different publication from the *Merck Manual*, the *Index* being an encyclopedia of chemicals. Here I found that if you had a hundred mice and gave them all 137 milligrams of caffeine per kilogram of body weight, half would die. This was cheerfully called LD 50, or lethal dose for fifty percent. My dictionary said a kilogram was 2.2 pounds. So if a man reacted like a mouse (although to me Ivor was more like a rat), that would work out to 13.7 grams of caffeine. Of course, getting thirteen grams of caffeine into the 220-plus pound Ivor was not going to happen, but then caffeine was not the only xanthine that was going to be going into Ivor.

A volume for the crime writer on poisons told me that one gram of caffeine could cause toxic symptoms, but it didn't tell me how much would kill. Well, if one gram was toxic, two grams ought to cause real trouble.

Now what about theobromine, the xanthine in chocolate? The *Merck Index* informed me that theobromine, "the principal alkaloid of the cacao bean," was a smooth muscle relaxant, diuretic, cardiac stimulant, and vasodilator. My, my! Sounded a lot like theophylline and caffeine. It said chocolate also contained some caffeine. That couldn't hurt.

How could I find out how much chocolate was dangerous? Certainly people eat large amounts with no ill effects. But at some point, with the other two xanthines . . . ?

I turned on my computer, thinking to get on the Net and ask how much theobromine there was in an average piece of dark bittersweet chocolate. But I held my hand back. This could be dangerous. I could be traced. Somewhere I had heard of people receiving catalogues from companies that sold items they had queried the Net about. Like travel brochures when they'd asked about tourist destinations or smoked salmon when they'd asked about where to get good fish. Webmasters could learn everything about you. I certainly didn't want anybody to know I was the person making queries about theobromine in chocolate. Could I ask anonymously? No. How could I be sure the query couldn't be traced?

Then I remembered the library at the local law school. If you looked like you belonged there, you could query databases at no charge, although there was a time limit. And there was a per-page charge if you wanted to print out what you found, but why should I want it in black and white? Now, if they just didn't ask for names. I grabbed my coat and ran out the door.

Two hours later I left the library highly pleased. I'd asked two databases to find articles that used "chocolate" within ten words of "theobromine" and got all kinds of good stuff. Chocolate, it seemed, frequently killed dogs. Dogs and cats didn't excrete the theobromine as well as humans. The poisoned animals would suffer rapid heart rates, muscle tremors, rapid respiration, convulsions, and even death.

Dark chocolate, I learned, contains ten times as much theobromine as milk chocolate. Bitter cooking chocolate contains 400 milligrams in an ounce! And—oh, yes!—the amount in a moderate amount of chocolate is about the same as the amount of caffeine in a moderate amount of coffee.

In humans, theobromine is a heart stimulant, smooth-muscle relaxant, and dilates coronary arteries. So what if we eliminate it faster than Rover would? It still had to have an additive effect with the other two.

All three of my drugs caused low blood pressure, irregular heart rhythm, sweating, convulsions, and, potentially, cardiac arrest. What's not to like? Ha! Take that! I thought. Hoist with your own petard.

The *PDR* had said that oral theophylline acted almost as swiftly as intravenous theophylline. But I knew I would need time to get a lot of coffee and chocolate into Ivor. He'd better not feel sick right away and just stop eating. Well, the desserts themselves should slow the absorption.

At this point in my research I phoned Sutcliffe and suggested we hold our rendezvous at Just Desserts.

When the day came and we sat down like two friends at Just Desserts, I encouraged Ivor to try the dense "flourless chocolate cake" first.

"It's excellent," I said. "Like a huge slice of dark chocolate. I'll have a piece myself." The waiter brought the cake promptly and filled our coffee with mocha java.

We tasted, nodded in appreciation, ate in companionable silence for a few minutes. Then I suggested he try the Turkish coffee, just for comparison, along with an almond-chocolate confection, for the blend of flavors. He agreed readily.

Now, since he was eating at my expense, he found the need to be borderline pleasant. "You know, I did say in the review that I've liked much of your past work."

Actually, no, you clot. His review of my first book, graven on my heart, said, "This novel is obviously the work of a beginner." And his review of my second book, also etched somewhere in my guts, said, "Ms. Grenfield has not yet got her sea legs for the mystery genre." The most recent review had, in fact, damned with faint praise: *This effort,* Snuffed, *is not up to her former standard.*

"Thank you," I said mildly.

"I suppose I should be frightened of eating with you, Ms. Grenfield. I've read so many novels where the central character, feeling wronged, invites his nemesis to dinner and poisons him."

"Well, Ivor, I was actually aware you might worry about that. I had thought of inviting you to my home. But it occurred to me that you might find it intimidating to be at the mercy of my cooking. Hence—Just Desserts."

Disarmed and possibly a little abashed, Sutcliffe said, "Well—you could hardly have found a more competent kitchen than this."

I nodded agreeably as Ivor finished his third cup of coffee—one regular, two Turkish so far—and pushed his cup within reach of the waiter. The calculator in my brain said that was 600 milligrams of caffeine now, give or take, and another two hundred on the way as the hot brew filled the cup.

Let's see. Add the capsule of theophylline just half an hour ago when he arrived. Didn't dare ask him the dosage, but it had to be either the standard 300 or the 400-milligram dose. Plus he had taken his morning dose, I supposed.

Ha! Well, me fine beauty, we'll just see how inartistic technology is. And we'll give you every chance to save yourself. Just a little paying of attention, Ivor. A morsel of humility.

Lord! That man could eat! *Schokoladenpudding,* which was a German chocolate-coffee-almond pudding served warm with whipped cream. *Rigo Jancsi* squares, dense Viennese cake that was more like frosting, which the waiter explained was named after a Gypsy violinist. And a slice of Sacher torte, a Viennese chocolate cake glazed with dark chocolate. *Shokoladno mindalnyi tort,* a Russian chocolate-almond torte made with rum, cinnamon, and, of all things, potato. Then just to be fair to the United States, he agreed to a simple fudge brownie with chocolate frosting, à la mode, as he put it, with coffee ice cream on the side. I had cherry strudel.

With each dessert he tried a different coffee. Ethiopian *sidamo,* Kenyan *brune,* a Ugandan dark roast. In my coffee reading I had noted that the *robusta* coffees have more than twice as much caffeine as the *arabica* species, and smiled indulgently as he drank some.

Two grams of caffeine by now, minimum. Clever of me to suggest he switch to the demitasses of various strong coffees. Just as strong and less filling. He could drink more of them.

Plus two to maybe four or five grams of theobromine from the chocolate.

"What are you working on these days, Ms. Grenfield?" Ivor said in his plummy voice. Could I detect a slight restless, hyper edge in his tone now?

"A mystery with historical elements," I answered, and almost giddy with delight, lobbed him a clue. "About Balzac and the discovery of some unknown, unpublished, very valuable manuscript." Balzac, of course, an avid, indeed compulsive coffee drinker, died of caffeine poisoning. Let's see if this self-important arbiter, this poseur, was any better at literature than he was at science.

"Oh, interesting," he drawled in boredom. "You know, I *could* just manage another dessert."

"Of course!" I caroled in glee. "How about a chocolate mousse? And another Turkish coffee to go with it." The waiter appeared, beaming. "And I'll have a vanilla cream horn."

"This is very pleasant," he said, chuckling as he plunged a spoon into his new dessert and gobbled the glob. "Actually, I'm rather surprised."

"Why?"

He became distracted, watching as another waiter passed with a silver tray of various chocolate candies on a lace doily—the house specialty, glossy dark, bittersweet chocolates with various fillings, handmade in their own kitchens. I raised a finger, said, "One of each for the gentleman," and pointed at Ivor. The waiter tenderly lifted the little beauties from the tray with silver tongs and placed them on a white china dish near Ivor's hand.

"Why surprised?" I reminded him.

He said, "I'd always thought of you as lacking in appreciation of the finer things."

"Oh, surely not."

"All those bloody and explicit murders, or poisons with their effects lovingly detailed. Hardly the work of a subtle mind."

"*Au contraire,* Ivor. I am very subtle."

"Well, I suppose it does require a certain amount of delicacy to keep the knowledge of whodunit from a reader until the end." He fidgeted as if nervous.

"Yes. Until the end."

Ivor began to cram the candies into his chunky, piggy cheeks. The pitch of his voice was rising, not louder but more shrill. Satiated, he pushed the dish away.

"Come on. Have another chocolate."

"I shouldn't."

"Oh, you only live once."

"Well, maybe just a taste or two." His fat hand, as he reached for the morsels, showed a faint tremor. He shifted his bulk. Restlessness.

Time for another clue, Ivor. Last chance, Ivor.

"Did you know that the botanical name for the cacao tree is Greek and that it translates to 'food of the gods'? *Theobroma,*" I said, trying not to chortle. Last chance, Ivor, you who know so much.

"Nope. Didn't know that. Rather apt, actually," he said without interest. He didn't care about this detail, either, didn't care how close to theophylline it sounded. His flushed face was a bit sweaty, seen in the subdued restaurant light. In fact, he looked as if he had been lightly buttered. He cleared his throat, took another swallow of coffee, and said, "Odd. I'm feeling a little short of breath."

"Your asthma?"

"Could be."

"That's too bad. Well, you know how to deal with it, anyhow."

"Ah—whew." Puff. "Yes."

"Well, shouldn't you do something? Don't you think you should take one of your pills?"

"I already did when I got here. The doc says don't exceed two per day."

"But that's a preventative dose, isn't it? If you have an attack coming on—?"

"Probably right." He groaned as he leaned his heavy bulk sideways to claw in his pocket for the pill vial. Wheezing harder, he drew it out. He tipped a capsule into his hand.

"Here," I said helpfully, and I pushed his cup of *robusta* coffee toward him. The waiter topped it up again.

"Hmmmp," was all the thanks he managed as he popped the pill and swallowed the java.

For another minute or so, Ivor sat still, catching his breath or whatever. His face was flushed, and he moved his head back and forth as if confused.

"Are you feeling all right, Ivor?"

"I may have eaten just a tad too much."

"Well, let's just sit awhile, then."

"Yes. Yes, we'll do that."

Ivor sat, but his hands twitched, then his fingers started to pleat and smooth the tablecloth. He took in deep breaths and let them out. His face was pinker still, almost the color of rare roast beef.

"I'm not sure about that tie you're wearing, Ivor," I said. "It's not up to your former standard."

Ivor goggled at me, but his bulging eyes were unfocused. He blew his cheeks out, then let them sag back, then blew them out again. His head began to bob up and down in a kind of tremor.

"And that suit," I said. "A fine well-bred wool. Quite incompatible with your character."

No answer. I said, "But perhaps that's a bit harsh."

He leaned forward, holding onto the table. Very slowly he drifted sideways, then faster and faster, until he fell off his chair, pulling the snowy white tablecloth, silver, forks and spoons, a china cup, the remains of brownie à la mode, and the dregs of *robusta* coffee with him.

"Oh, my goodness!" I shouted.

The waiter came running. I fanned Ivor with a menu. "Stand back. Give him air," I said. The waiter stepped back obediently.

The manager came running also. He tried the Heimlich maneuver. No luck. Several diners stood up and gawked. Ivor was making bubbling, gasping sounds.

"That's not a fainting fit," the manager said, obviously a more analytical chap than the waiter.

"I guess not," I said.

The manager wrung his hands. "What should we do? What should we do?"

"Maybe it's an asthma attack. He carries some pills for it. They're in his pocket, I think."

The manager felt in Ivor's pocket. He read the label. A

genuine doctor's prescription in a real pharmacy container. "Yes. Here they are. At least they can't hurt."

"This coffee is cool enough," I said. "Wash it down with this." He did, even though Ivor choked a lot and showed no awareness of what was going on.

"Call the paramedics," the manager told the waiter, who bustled away. The manager slapped Ivor's cheek. I envied the man this role, but had to stand by. Ivor produced no reaction to being slapped, now well and truly in a coma.

The paramedics arrived with reasonable promptness. The one with the box of medical supplies knelt by Ivor to take vital signs. The second said, "What can you tell us about this? What happened?"

I shook my head. "I can't imagine. He was just eating a perfectly delicious chocolate dessert."

Ivor gasped, but did not rouse. His cheeks were taking on a purplish hue, the color of a fine old burgundy.

I thought of the last line of Ivor Sutcliffe's review:

In Snuffed, *the only thing deader than Rufus Crown is Ms. Grenfield's plot.*

Some things take time. Some of the best things take quite a lot of time.

Dolley Madison

and the Staff of Life

"Amelia, would you pass the president the condiments?" Dolley Madison said. She had observed her husband's slightly impatient glance as it swept the luncheon table. He could be irritable when his gastronomic needs were not met. As the girl carried the cruets to James' end of the table, Dolley added, "I'm quite worried that the ambassador will find us provincial here."

They were expecting the new Russian ambassador, just assigned to Washington, at a dinner this evening.

"They may find many things provincial here, Dolley. And about that we can do nothing. But one thing they will not find provincial is you."

She smiled. Really he could be quite delightful.

James returned to a subject on which he had been speaking earlier. "It is all very well for the Northern states to criticize the slow growth of trade and industry. It is always easy to complain. But the development of a nation's industry follows its own course, to a degree. It grows at a natural pace, from elements such as the availability of raw materials and skillful workers which develop together. It cannot be rushed more than a judicious amount. It requires a proper passage of time to mature."

"I'm sure that's true, James," said Dolley, sighing faintly.

"Where is my cider?"

"The cider is not ready, James."

"I wanted cider."

21

"This is October first, dear. We always make the first pressing in early October when the winter apples are ripe. As you have said yourself, summer apples make a cider that's not worth drinking."

"I like cider with my luncheon."

"And after the pressing, it requires three days in a cool room for proper fermentation to take place. Like the industry of a nation, it requires a proper passage of time to mature."

"How much longer will it be?"

"Well, I did have six barrels moved to the warm room so as to mature more quickly. They should be drinkable tomorrow."

"I suppose that will have to do."

Dolley sighed a second time.

Then she noticed a tear splash on the polished table.

Amelia stood there with the platter of smoked fish. Dolley looked up at the girl. Tears were welling in her eyes, even though she bit her lip and tried to, appear composed. "Why, child, what's wrong?" Dolley said.

Amelia burst into sobs.

James said, "Dolley, the conduct of the household staff is your responsibility."

Amelia ran from the room.

Dolley Madison drew Amelia into a corner of the service pantry. The silver and china were stored here. There were no kitchens inside the White House. Kitchens, ovens, rooms to hang meat, rooms to ferment beverages, to allow bread to rise, or to store vegetables, were all outside the White House in small warm rooms or cold rooms so that neither their odors nor the heat of ovens in summer would seep into the mansion itself.

"We can't have this, Amelia," Dolley said.

"Oh, I am so sorry, Ma'am," the girl sobbed. Service at the White House was a choice position, and she didn't want to lose it. In addition, she liked the First Lady, even if the president frightened her.

"What has so upset you?"

"I have accepted George's proposal of marriage."

"I see. When?"

"I told him just a few minutes ago."

Dolley cocked her head and thought. George Fredericks was an unpleasant, hotheaded young man, but he was head butler, in charge of the White House silver. Amelia truly loved Henry Poole, who was a lowly supplies porter. Amelia's family, over the last several weeks, had remorselessly urged her to accept George, and in the last day or two had virtually ordered her to do so.

"It is not my place to interfere with your parents' counsel, dear," Dolley said at last. But she contrived to add, "Possibly a long engagement might be wise."

It was an hour and a half later when the head ostler and the chief of White House staff bustled into the entry hall. They wished to see the president, but he was closeted with a delegation from Massachusetts and Dolley intercepted them.

"Henry Poole has been found dead, Ma'am," the chief of staff said.

"Oh, no! Where?"

"Near the grape arbor. Not far from the stables."

"Show me."

They hesitated, but as she held firm, they finally complied.

Henry Poole lay on the turned earth near the roots of a grapevine. "How long do you suppose he has been dead?" Dolley asked.

"It's warm here in the sun, Ma'am. Therefore, the temperature of the body is not a good guide. And he has . . . ah . . . has—"

"Become rigid?" Dolley asked, wondering yet another time how it was that men thought women had no idea of the facts of life.

"Yes, Ma'am. But that is quite a variable effect. I should say between one and three hours, Ma'am."

"You have noticed the injury on his forehead?"

"Yes, Ma'am."

"It suggests a murderous attack. Notify whatever authorities are appropriate. Keep me constantly informed."

Dolley Madison, of course, was thinking of George Fredericks. One could hardly think of an attack on Henry Poole without thinking of George Fredericks. But the circumstances were certainly very peculiar.

She found George in the pantry and immediately taxed him with it.

"I never attacked Henry," was his first response.

"You have reddened knuckles. There is an abrasion on your chin. There was bad blood between you. Don't make me impatient with you."

When Dolley Madison became emphatic, it was hard to resist her. She watched George think, his jaw working unattractively for half a minute. Then he said, "He attacked me, Ma'am. I was only defending myself."

"Tell me the circumstances."

"Amelia accepted my proposal of marriage. I had gone out to the supplies shed to see if the soft polishing cloths had been left there by mistake. He saw me cross the yard. He began to berate me about the betrothal, and we went into the warm-room outbuilding to argue. He attacked me there. We fought. We bumped into the table where the bread was and knocked some pans onto the floor. We bumped into two of the cider kegs and knocked them over. During the course of the fight,

Henry struck his head. But he was not unconscious, and he walked away, only staggering somewhat. I remained behind to pick up the bread pans and set the cider kegs upright. No cider was spilled, Ma'am. I can say that. Henry must have walked some distance and collapsed and died, for I swear I never saw him after he went out the door. And I didn't wish to see him anymore, so I did not look for him."

Dolley immediately went to the warm room.

It was a long, separate outbuilding, kept warm with a small Franklin stove. Down the center ran trestle tables on which bread was set to rise, or, in the winter, on which frozen supplies from unheated outbuildings were set to thaw. The kegs of cider that she had designated were next to the tables, fermenting a bit faster than was truly advisable. The pans of bread had already been removed, no doubt to the ovens for baking. The dinner for the Russian ambassador was now just a few hours off.

Understanding all of what had happened, Dolley decided it was time to tell the president. It was their custom to take tea at midafternoon. This would be a good opportunity.

Amelia was not serving at tea. Dolley had given her leave to spend the afternoon in her room.

The president listened as Dolley explained the circumstances of the death. "George says he was defending himself against attack, which is less reprehensible than attacking Henry, of course," she concluded.

"Indeed it is. Far less. The second is murder."

"But it cannot have happened as he claims."

"Certainly it could. It makes perfect sense in view of the individuals involved. George is hotheaded, and surely would strike back if attacked. And it makes no sense that *he* would instigate an attack on *Henry*, after Amelia had accepted him and made him the victor in their suit for her hand."

"She accepted him just before serving our luncheon. But Henry cannot have been killed after that."

"Why not?"

"His account of the fight is wrong. As I see it, Amelia met Henry before luncheon, probably in the warm room, to tell him she planned to accept George, as her family wished. Amelia and Henry were in love, and they parted with great sadness, perhaps a gesture or two of affection."

"They ought not waste working time—"

"Please, James! I think George must have come upon them—or perhaps followed her from the house—and, not knowing she planned to accept his suit, seeing them together became enraged. He must have bided his time, though, until Amelia left, because she did not see him attack Henry, and later told him she would marry him. But as soon as she was gone, he struck. He is, as you say, a hothead. In any case, he did not strike in defense of himself."

"But equally a hothead before luncheon and after. You cannot possibly know, Dolley, which time it was."

"Yes, I can. The bread pans could only have been knocked off the table without the bread being ruined, before luncheon, while the dough was still dense and low in the pan. By early afternoon, it would have risen over the top. And indeed it had already gone to the ovens when I went to inspect the warm house. Even tipping a pan on its side once the bread is risen and fragile, would have ruined the loaf."

"I see."

"Bread, like industry and cider and love, is a commodity that requires the proper passage of time to mature."

The film vamps from the early black and white movie days were often a little bit creepy. In the days of silent films, Theda Bara was the ultimate seductress, the woman of mystery. One of the many things said about her was that her name spelled backwards (almost) was Arab Death. In the 1930s, the dawn of the "talkies," the great Hollywood woman of mystery was Greta Garbo. When Ed Gorman asked me to write a celebrity story for his collection Celebrity Vampires, *I chose Ms. Garbo. To me she always seemed unreal . . .*

I Vant to Be Alone

It was that in-between time of day the French call *l'heure bleu.* There was a blue-gray haze of humid air over Central Park and a sooty haze over the rest of the city. From where I stood, I could see all the way across the park, and the buildings on the west might have been a charcoal sketch done on rough paper. No air stirred. New York was marinating in its own exhaust.

The Upper East Side was as hot as the rest of the city, despite being fashionable and expensive. Tonight was identical to a hundred other July evenings here, and yet night would never be the same again.

Yesterday, man had landed on the moon.

As I crossed Fifth Avenue, I looked at the sky. I wasn't sure whether this would be a night for a full moon or not. Because I had been doing background reading on my assignment, I had not had time to look up the phases of the moon, and it didn't matter anyway. What mattered was that night would never be the same. I stood on the pavement, a young earthbound man who might some day walk on the moon. The universe was less mysterious, perhaps, and to me more appalling.

I couldn't quite get a fix on how I felt about it. The human race had now gone far beyond the so-called discovery of the new world by the Europeans. After all, the new world was new only to the Europeans themselves, in their self-centeredness. The Maya, the Inca, the Eskimo, and the Native Americans had been there all along.

No, landing on the moon was far more than a giant step; it was wholly new.

And yet, there was something horrifying about it to me. Something dreadful—a metastasis of a sort. As if killer bees, previously confined to Africa, had come ashore in Florida in the luggage hold of an airliner. Or as if the beetle that carried Dutch elm disease were arriving in New York harbor in a piece of imported wood. Was mankind now to infect the entire universe?

For God's sake, what was the matter with me? I was on the verge of the scoop of my career, if I could bring it off. I was, as the British put it, "over the moon." That was an expression that would probably go by the wayside now, I guess, signifying, as it did, happiness beyond your wildest dreams.

Actually, I forgot about this peculiar angst and reverted to my normal personality when I stepped into the lobby of the building on the Upper East Side. Evening had darkened into night. The excitement of the upcoming interview bubbled in my blood, and the portentousness was added to by the elegance of the beautifully constructed building. Besides, I was young and feisty and hardheaded and pretty brash, too, the very model of the up-and-coming reporter. It was twenty-four years ago. I was twenty-seven.

Imagine being twenty-seven!

I had expected to be admitted by a butler in black or a maid dressed in gray with a white lace apron. Anything but what happened. The door was opened wide and there she stood.

That face, the enthralling face—as beautiful today at sixty-four as when she made *Anna Christie* at the age of twenty-five. Twenty-eight years since her last picture, and she was as famous as she had ever been. The deep-set eyes, the chiseled planes of cheek, that clean, firm line of chin. This was beauty that struck one dumb, and I couldn't speak. Me! Speechless!

"Mr. Briskman?" she said. Yes, the husky voice, slightly accented, very sensual.

"Hal Briskman, Miss Garbo."

She did not use my first name, though (callow youth!) I had half hoped she would. In fact, she didn't say anything at all, but stepped back, closed the door behind me, and led me into a wide living room.

"I have brought a tape recorder, Miss Garbo. Is that all right? I wanted to be precise when I quoted you."

"Quite all right."

She sat down and gestured to an adjacent chair. Then—nothing. She merely sat and watched me, watched intently and rather eagerly.

I was fully prepared, with three steno-pad pages of questions. I was always prepared in those days, knowing perfectly well I couldn't count on experience or craft.

"Uh—I don't especially want to go over parts of your personal history that have been written about frequently. Unless, that is, you want to tell me more about them. Add something." I looked at her. She merely watched. But she didn't object.

"Your father was an unskilled laborer, who died when you were young, I think?"

"Yes."

"You grew up in Stockholm." In a very poor district, but I didn't quite want to put it that way.

"Yes."

"Your first job was as a lather girl in a barber shop. Because someone noticed your beauty, you were given a role in an advertising film."

"Yes. It was sheer chance." She glanced from me to the room we sat in, reflecting, I suppose, that all this luxury was also the fruit of sheer chance. As was life, perhaps.

"Mauritz Stiller, the Swedish director, discovered you in 1924."

"Yes." For a moment I thought this would be another of her monosyllabic answers, but her eyes took on that hundred-mile gaze, like the last scene in *Queen Christina*, and she said, "He taught me everything. Everything."

She and he were always together; he was Svengali to her Trilby. He introduced her to artistic society, trained her dramatic skills, and even ran her professional business life.

"Then," I said, "Louis B. Mayer offered Stiller a Hollywood job in 1924, but Stiller insisted that you be given a contract as well."

"Yes."

"And you came together to the United States. Mayer, foolishly, didn't want to hire you, but he gave in."

Her head bent toward me. "Do you know what he said? Mayer said, 'American men don't like fat women.' "

"I heard about that."

"They wanted me ethereal, transparent. They thought I was big and awkward."

"But you filmed as ethereal."

"Yes, exactly. On the film," she said, her attention fixed closely on me.

"*The Torrent* showed how tremendously effective you were

in front of the camera. But off-camera, in the midst of the Hollywood publicity storm, you were already developing a reputation for being noncommunicative."

"Yes. They believed it was because of my accent."

I waited in case she would tell me what the reason really as, if it wasn't the accent, but when the silence drew out, finally said, "Then in 1927 Stiller went home to Sweden without you."

"Yes," she said, and those deep-sunken eyelids drooped.

How to ask about her romances? I said, "Your name was linked romantically with John Gilbert during the filming of *Flesh and the Devil.*"

"Yes." Was that a faint smile?

"And later with Leopold Stokowski, and the director Rouben Mamoulian, even the famous health guru Gaylord Hauser and the photographer Cecil Beaton."

No answer at all. Now I was determined not to go on to the next question, to let the silence lengthen out until she *had* to say something, to give me a quotable line about one of the men.

But she didn't. After some time she said, "Do you know what someone called me? 'The dream princess of eternity.' "

She turned her face full to me and waited for my reaction.

I was stumped. Finally, thinking I sounded like a psychiatrist, I said, "Did you like it when they said that, or not?"

"Actually, I thought it was rather appropriate."

Another silence, not awkward really, but strung tight, like a filament of spiderweb.

"You were just about the only silent star who made a successful transition to sound. And you were spectacularly successful. For *Anna Christie*, as you know, of course, the ads were 'Garbo Talks!' Did it worry you, the change to sound?"

"No."

"And then *Ninotchka.* 'Garbo laughs!' "

"Yes."

Every aspect of her body—gestures, facial expressions, tone of voice—conveyed reticence. This didn't surprise me, as her shyness was legendary. And yet, she had agreed to the interview. What surprised me was a sort of hunger that went with the aloofness, an approach/avoidance. I put it down to her having been alone too long.

"Have you ever wanted to do another film?"

She took this very seriously, considering it for some time and answering more slowly than before. Finally she said, "Oh, no. I think I am now much too ethereal."

"You were twice voted best actress of the year by the New York film critics. Did you find that validating? Did it please you?"

"Somewhat."

"But you didn't receive an Oscar until 1954 when they gave you a special Oscar. Were you annoyed at being passed over earlier?"

"No."

I sighed. So many monosyllabic answers. I wasn't worried, really. I was here, in her apartment. I had spoken to the Enigma, the woman who went out, when she went out at all, heavily dressed in flowing coats and capes, with scarves over her head, the woman who had said she lived alone with a bar of soap and one toothbrush. Photographers and reporters descend upon her everywhere she goes, but none has ever gotten close enough for a close-up shot. People simply did not see her. But I had, only me, and it would be a coup, whatever she said. Still, I wanted some comment, some quote I could call my own.

I sighed again, shifted my weight, and may have made a move that looked like I was thinking of leaving.

At any rate, she seemed to realize that, if she was to keep my interest, she had to be more forthcoming. "Mauritz Stiller was the finest director I ever knew," she said.

"But he didn't stay on in Hollywood."

"No. What a shame that was. He was too impulsive. His directorial style was too changeable. The set was forever in an uproar. They had no idea how to tell whether he was getting the work done, although they should have known he would because he had in the past. He had made wonderful films. Hollywood wanted its movies produced like Fords, on a production line."

She moved closer, emphasizing her words with her eyes.

"Mauritz Stiller changed the whole direction of my life."

She was wearing something silk, I think, that brushed against itself with the sound that moth wings might make, on night air.

I said, "Why did you agree to talk with me?"

"It is pleasant to see someone young. Someone who is youthful and vigorous. I spend so much time with men and women who are gray and worn. Older people. It is pleasant to speak with someone who is so, so robust."

The lights took on an amber undertone. Like the color of honey. Her voice, an odd, quirky, low voice, held all the thick sweetness of honey. There was a humming in my ears.

I looked at my steno pad for reassurance. But how silly! Why did I need reassurance? There was my last major prepared question for her—indeed the Big Question. She had retired quite suddenly. She had never returned to film, nor even to public life. It had long been speculated that her retirement was the result not only of shyness, not only because she grew "tired of making faces," though she was certainly shy, but also because her last movie, *Two-Faced Woman*, made in 1941, was badly received by the critics and public both. I had left this for last for fear that she would be insulted and terminate the interview. I opened my mouth to ask her. I fully believed I was going to ask her that question.

Two-Faced Woman.

She moved closer to me.

"Well, thank you, Miss Garbo," was what my mouth said. "I don't want to exhaust my welcome." I rose abruptly to my feet.

She seemed puzzled. When I stood, she stood, too, and walked graciously with me to the door.

This was not a woman of impulse, and yet it seemed like an impulsive confidence when she said, "They wanted an ethereal woman. They wanted a woman who was young, and ageless, too, and with the wisdom of ages."

In a brief seventeen-year career of acting in American films, Greta Garbo had become the most famous of the screen goddesses. But she was always aloof, and always a mystery. And I have never, not so much as for one full day, ceased to wonder about that interview and about her. Who and what was she?

She said once, "I am a misfit in the world."

I'm fifty-one now; the next milestone will be sixty. I think more and more about the Isaac Watts line, "Time, like an ever rolling stream, bears all her sons away." I am being borne away, slowly, on a gentle river. And I wonder, sometimes.

What would a person do, what would a woman risk, to become an international star?

And would it be worth it?

The interview was, as I had expected, the coup of my career. Looking back on it, probably the foundation of my career. Because of that interview, just my unadorned report on how she looked and the literal reproduction of what she had said, I had a call to the *New York Times*, which gave me a boost to a higher position on the *Chicago Tribune*, which led finally to my present position, editor in chief at *Chicago Today*. Without that interview, I suspect none of this would have happened. Journalism is like a pyramid with a very wide bottom and a very narrow top. There are thousands and thousands of bright young reporters scrambling upward like termites, but they don't make it without at least one break.

Who was she? The Eternal Vamp.

An actress and a beautiful woman. That's all and that's enough.

I think, really, I was just in an odd frame of mind that night. There was in fact no subtext to our conversation, and my belief, fleeting even then, that she was—that she had another reality she was trying to tell me about—all that was a product of the oddness of that night. Man had walked on the moon, and I was primed for strangeness. The nature of the world had changed. I was moonstruck.

I'm really quite sure.

This story takes place on a real day during a real event, the great Chicago Valentine's Day Blizzard of 1990. About three in the afternoon, just before rush hour, cars began to bog down in falling snow. As they sat there, some ran out of gas and very soon nobody could move, anywhere in the city. Even the snowplows could not get through. It was several days before the city thawed.

Hard Feelings

Officer Susannah Maria Figueroa was frightened, and she hated being frightened. It made her angry. Even worse, she was sure her partner Norm Bennis felt horrible, too. Nevertheless, he had made a serious mistake, and his mistake had gotten them both into trouble.

Suze Figueroa sat on one side of the waiting room, her arms folded across her chest. Far away in the other corner— as far away from her as he could get and still be in the same room—sat Norm Bennis, feet spread, elbows on knees, hands dangling, head hanging. He looked absolutely miserable.

Hell, Suze thought, he ought to. She just hoped he felt guilty as hell, making a stupid mistake and then sticking with it. Stubborn bastard!

But they'd been together so long!

Bennis was her mentor and her friend.

The Police Academy teaches you what they think you need to know. Then the job—and your partner—teach you what you really need to know. Suze Figueroa had been assigned to Bennis just after she finished the initial on-the-job phase of working with a supervisor. She'd been afraid of what Norm would think of her at first. He looked so solid and experienced—like a walking ad for professionalism in police work for the twenty-first century. He'd been ten years a Chicago cop when she came on. He was built like a wedge, with narrow hips, a broad chest, and very wide shoulders. His square brown face, when she first saw it at that first roll call, was set in a scowl. But she soon realized that he thought it was lots of fun being mentor to a five-foot-one-inch naive female.

They hit it off immediately, and Bennis never made fun of her for not knowing whether a ten-young or a one-frank was a "disturbance, domestic, peace restored" or a "dog bite, report filed." He didn't belittle her, as her trainer sometimes had, for not knowing how to fill out a specific form. He knew the department didn't run on gas or electricity, it ran on paper, and he knew when she'd filled out a couple hundred of them, she would remember all the forms.

Bennis was sardonic, but not sour.

For her part, Suze teased him about the long series of women who took his fancy for about three weeks apiece, but she sympathized too. She was divorced. Her ex-husband called her the "affirmative-action cop." By this he meant that she was too short and too female to be any good to anybody.

Bennis thought she was just fine on the job. "You back me up better than any partner I've ever had."

"Hey, Bennis! I'm not just backup. I'm forefront."

"That too."

Suze and Norm and half the First District went to the Furlough Bar for a beer after a tour. Recently, Suze and Norm had taken to going to an occasional movie instead. It was not exactly a girl-and-boy thing, Suze told herself. They were both too embarrassed at the thought of being called just another squad car romance.

And now—now they wouldn't even look at each other.

★ ★ ★ ★ ★

It was 11 A.M. on February 15, the day after the incident. Two rooms down the hall, a roundtable of inquiry—four men and one woman, including an assistant deputy superintendent, a state's attorney, and the union rep—were reviewing the documents in the case. They had before them the fire department reports and the preliminary findings of the medical examiner and the detectives. But the reports from other departments only explained what happened after the incident. After the point where Norm's story and Suze Figueroa's story diverged.

Their commander, Sazerac, sat with them in the waiting room. He was as unhappy as they were. Finally he spoke.

"There's no way I can stop this. But it bothers me. I wouldn't have figured you for a shirker, Figueroa."

"What do you mean?"

"Don't you realize how they see this?"

"Yes, boss. They know that Bennis and I have two different stories about last night, and so they think one of us is improperly describing the case. So they think one of us is lying. Which would be a reprimand."

"No, Figueroa. It's not that minor."

"Minor! I've never had a reprimand and I don't intend to have one now! Uh. Sir."

Sazerac sighed. "Listen to me. We're talking separation from the department. Maybe prosecution."

"For what?"

"They think you left that man to die in the fire, Figueroa. And made up your story later to cover up. To make it seem he was dead."

Bennis groaned. "But he *was* dead, sir! Figueroa would never—"

"And they think you, Bennis, added that diagnosis later,

after you realized that your story cast doubt on whether he was dead."

"That's not true. I said he was dead when I wrote it up this morning."

"Not strongly. You 'thought he was dead.' They figure that you said it more strongly later because the two of you have gotten together to save her ass."

"No. No, sir. That's just not true. Sir, Figueroa is the best officer I've ever worked with. She'd never abandon a living person."

"Are you reconsidering *your* testimony, Bennis?"

Bennis looked from Suze Figueroa to the commander and back. His face was anguished. "I can't. I'm sorry, Figueroa. I can't lie. Maybe I was temporarily disoriented by the fire. But I have to say what I know. I can't lie."

"You're lying now, Bennis," she said. "I wish I knew why."

Figueroa was seething. Bennis stared away from her at the dead plant in the corner. The commander sighed again, and then sat silent.

The door opened. A man in uniform came one step into the room. "The board is ready for you," he said.

"It was one of those nights that a lot of people call 'real Chicago weather,' " Suze Figueroa said to the board. "It had started to snow at about three in the afternoon, just as Officer Bennis and I came on duty. We knew immediately that the rush hour was going to be hell—uh, was going to be very difficult. People had started coming into town, too, for Valentine's Day dinners. By four o'clock it was snowing so hard you couldn't see across the street. By five there were already cars backed up spinning their wheels on the steeper access ramps to Lake Shore Drive and the Kennedy Expressway.

Some of them had run out of gas, blocking the streets, and would be there until Streets and San made it through to tow them."

She was trying to hold in her fear, trying to put out of her mind the thought that she might be fired. Being a cop was what she had always wanted.

"It was constant from the moment we hit the street. We picked people out of stalled cars who were too scared to get out. We found several street people and ran them to shelters. We—"

The ADS, Wardron, chopped her description short. "Officer Figueroa," he said, "get to the incident."

"Yes, sir. But the weather played a very large part—"

"We know what the weather was last night. Move forward."

"Yes, sir." This guy Wardron was going to be trouble, she thought. He looked like Mike Ditka and used his voice like the blade of a guillotine. She had vibes, sometimes, when she felt sure that another cop didn't like women on the department. She didn't want to think that this guy was out to get her, personally and specifically, but she'd bet if he could prove that some woman cop had run scared, he'd enjoy doing it.

"At 2140 hours we got a call. . . ."

"One thirty-three," the radio had said. They were car thirty-three in the First District. Since Figueroa was driving, Bennis picked up and said, "Thirty-three."

"Woman screaming for help at eight-one-seven west on Chestnut."

"You got a floor on that, squad?"

"On the two."

"Caller give a name?"

"Oh, yeah. Citizen. Concerned citizen."

"I know the guy well."

"Gal."

"Whatever."

Because of the snow, all the usual city sounds around them were muffled. In fact, there were virtually no automobile noises, and they heard the dispatcher more clearly than usual. No need to repeat. Bennis said, "Ten-four."

The snow had filled the streets and was still coming down. Figueroa said, "Jeez, Bennis. It's not the traction that's a problem. It's all the abandoned cars."

"You can get around 'em here if you drive on the sidewalk."

"Right."

"Don't clip the fire hydrant."

"Bennis, please! You know what an excellent driver I am."

"Figueroa, my man, I'd trust you with my life. In fact, I do it on a daily basis."

"And you're still alive, too."

"Watch out for the dumpster!"

"Missed it by a mile."

"A good quarter of an inch anyhow."

The radio said: *"One thirty-three."*

"Thirty-three."

"We got a second call on that woman screaming for help. Where are you?"

"Northbound on LaSalle. Driving's real bad, squad," Bennis said, trying not to gasp as Figueroa slowed within kissing distance of a light pole. "But I'd guess we're just two minutes out now."

"Yeah, thirty-three. Okay. By the way, the news is it's gonna keep snowing until noon tomorrow."

"How nice."

Bennis and Figueroa pulled up in front. They had entered

thousands of buildings, not knowing what they'd find. They relied on each other. Each knew that the other would be there, and they even had their own shorthand way of communicating. Bennis pointed a finger to show Figueroa that it was her turn to stand to the far side of the apartment door. Then he knocked. But before he could knock again, Figueroa pointed. "Look."

There was smoke coming out around the top of the door.

Bennis felt the door to see if it was cool, which it was. The last thing he wanted was to start a backdraft. Then he backed up to take a kick at the door. But that instant it opened and a man came running out. His hair and jacket were on fire, and he was screaming. He didn't even see the two cops, but crashed frantically down the stairs.

Bennis spun and went after him, knowing Figueroa would put out the emergency call to the dispatcher. He raced down the stairs three at a time and still couldn't catch up with the terrified man until, leaping, screaming down the cement steps outside the front door, the man fell. The fire on his hair and jacket had spread. Bennis rolled him over in the snow three or four times. Then, thinking to chill the charred flesh and prevent further burn damage, he grabbed up handfuls of snow and slapped it all over the man's head and back.

There was no time to wait and see how badly hurt the man was. God only knew how many people were in the building. Bennis bolted back inside and up the stairs.

Meanwhile, Figueroa had keyed her radio. "One thirty-three, emergency."

"Go ahead, thirty-three."

"There's a fire in this apartment, and it's going fast."

"I'll get the smokies."

" 'Four."

Talking on her radio had used just six seconds. At the

same time, she had been scanning the apartment. She could hardly see anything, the smoke was so thick, but she heard a woman screaming. Figueroa dropped to her hands and knees and crawled fast toward the screams.

She found herself in the kitchen, where a woman, standing up, was rushing into a broom closet, falling down when she hit the wall, rushing in again, terrified and convinced it was the front door.

Figueroa grabbed her. "Get out of my way!" the woman screamed over and over.

Figueroa said, "Hey! Stop it!"

"Get out of my way!"

Figueroa slapped her.

The flames were running along the floorboards now. The woman kept shrieking.

"Come with me, god-dammit!" Figueroa seized the woman's hand, pulled her to the floor. She put her arm over the woman's shoulder and hustled her on all fours toward the front door.

This woman was burned already, Figueroa thought. Her skin felt hot to the touch, and Figueroa could almost believe she felt blisters starting to form.

Pushing and cajoling and bullying, she got the woman into the living room. Crossing the floor, she realized she was crawling over the body of a man lying there unmoving, but she didn't have time to worry about that. She got the woman to the door.

The hall was still cool and the air in it was fresh, so she pushed the woman out and yelled after her, "Warn your neighbors."

There was no time to make sure she did. Suze Figueroa saw Bennis coming up the stairs. She yelled, "There's a man inside."

On hands and knees she crawled back in, touching the hot wall to make sure where she was going. She found the man, but at the same instant she and Bennis heard a baby start to scream. Bennis was next to her now and he slapped the man's cheek, but the man didn't move.

Figueroa felt the man's forehead. Smoke swirled above him, but he was lifeless and cold. The baby screamed louder, from a back bedroom.

"I gotta get the kid," she said to Bennis. She wasn't sure he could hear over the roar of the fire, but then she found him following her as they crawled to the bedroom.

"How many kids?" she yelled.

There was just one crib.

Bennis stood up, grabbed a little girl out of the crib, put her solidly under one arm, and ran like a quarterback for the front door. Suze stayed to check for another child.

The fire was flashing across the ceiling now. She didn't have much time.

One crib. *Hurry up!* No other child's bed. No crying. *Hurry! It's hot!* As far as she could see through the smoke, only girl-child toys in one age group—two soft dolls, one stuffed bear, a play muffin tin, and some plastic spoons. One child.

Part of the ceiling fell.

Taking a last breath of air from floor level, Figueroa jumped up and bolted for the front door. The living room was a hell of flame, and if she hadn't memorized where the door was, she would never have made it. Her hair was singed. She could not even see the man on the floor. He was dead, anyway, and she had to warn the upstairs neighbors.

Outside, fire engines were fighting their way through streets blocked with stalled cars. They didn't arrive until ten minutes later.

★ ★ ★ ★ ★

"I want to point out," Commander Sazerac said to Deputy Wardron, "that Officers Bennis and Figueroa got the other tenants out of the building. Which, given the weather and the time it took for the fire battalion to arrive, surely saved their lives."

"We understand that," Wardron said, clipping his words.

Sazerac said, "The building was totally involved when the fire engines arrived. And then they had trouble getting water to it. Stalled cars were blocking the fire hydrants."

"We are aware of that."

"When the fire was finally struck at 0330 hours, Officers Bennis and Figueroa were still caring for residents, even though they were four and a half hours past the end of their tour."

"Commander Sazerac, I appreciate your attempt to help your men—ah, people—but we are interested in what happened in the Molitor apartment, not what happened afterward. We'll proceed."

Bennis said angrily, "I personally saw Officer Figueroa rescue six residents from the upper floors."

"Officer Bennis, we'll get your story later."

Commander Sazerac said loudly, "And she was burned in the attempt, Deputy!"

"Not relevant now. We'll take it into account during sentencing."

"Don't you mean *if* there is a decision to go to sentencing, Deputy?"

"Of course, Commander. This is just a preliminary roundtable. My mistake." He turned his head and addressed the four board members. "We will note Commander Sazerac has questions about this process. However, we will take matters up in order. We are not going to use this process today as a way for the two officers involved to get their stories straight between them."

Commander Sazerac said, "They could have done that at any time in the last twelve hours. It's their integrity and their unwillingness to alter their reports to say the same thing that has caused a difference in perception to be blown up into this silly—"

"Commander! This is a fact-finding proceeding. It is an inappropriate time to make arguments. Hold them until the charges have been proven or not proven."

Wardron was in charge here, not Sazerac. Departmental structure being what it was, there was nothing Sazerac could do but sit by, just about as useful as the photo of the superintendent on the wall.

He and Wardron held each other's eyes for two or three seconds.

Figueroa said, "Sir, may I ask what the circumstances were that led up to the fire? We came into a situation midway—"

"Which is no excuse."

"I'm not suggesting that it is. But the fire obviously started in that apartment, and there were three adults inside who didn't seem to have made any effort to put it out. Why was Mr. Molitor lying in the middle of the living room floor? If he'd been shot, for instance, I would think I'd be entitled to know that. It certainly wasn't the smoke that killed him. He was down on the floor where the air was good."

"I don't suppose there's any reason not to tell you. We have a reasonably full picture, from the statement of the woman and the statements of the neighbors."

The Molitors had begun fighting in the afternoon—a husband, his wife, and the wife's brother. Fighting and drinking, and drinking and fighting. Among the burned remnants of their apartment were dozens of beer cans and the fragments of two bottles that had contained scotch.

By early evening, the neighbors were getting pretty tired of it. Judging by their observations and the wife's story, about nine the husband, who until then had been just shouting and threatening and hitting the wall with his fists, started hitting his wife. She hit back for a while, then fell, and he kicked her. She screamed for help and one of the neighbors, too frightened to go in or knock, called the police.

Meanwhile, the brother had come to the wife's defense. He attacked the husband, who by now was in a blind rage. The husband pushed the brother, who fell over the wife, and then the husband grabbed a can of lighter fluid, ran wild, spraying it along the living room and kitchen walls, and lighted it. The brother surged up off the floor. The wife, terrified, crawled to what she thought was the front door, but she was dazed from several blows, and now smoke was filling the room, and she actually went into the kitchen.

Meanwhile, the brother had picked up a chair and hit the husband over the head, hard. The husband went down.

At about this point, Figueroa and Bennis were pulling up outside. The brother's hair had caught fire. He panicked and ran out of the apartment, where he was intercepted by Bennis.

Wardron continued: "Officer Figueroa, what you should have done after Officer Bennis left with the baby was to attempt to get Mr. Molitor out. You might not have succeeded, but you should have tried."

"I knew the man on the floor was dead. He was cold."

"Officer Bennis, was he cold?"

Bennis swallowed. Figueroa fixed him with her eyes, but he didn't look at her. For a moment he straightened up, squaring his shoulders, as if he were steeling himself to take action. Then his face sagged.

"He was still warm," he said.

Commander Sazerac asked, "Isn't there a way to tell whether he was dead before the fire got to him? You should be able to test for carbon sucked into the lungs. If he wasn't breathing—"

"Commander Sazerac, we appreciate your help," Wardron said, in a tone that made it clear that he didn't. "Believe it or not, we thought of that."

Sazerac watched sourly. He knew there was something wrong with the way they were getting the picture, but he couldn't put his finger on where the problem was. Figueroa would not have left a living man to burn to death. Sazerac had been a commander much too long to make serious mistakes in judgment about his officers' characters. There was a problem with Figueroa, but it was the opposite. Like a lot of short female officers, she had a tendency to put herself in harm's way unnecessarily and play Jane Wayne. This charge against her was dead wrong.

Wardron added, "The entire building was engulfed when the fire department finally made it. Shortly after that, the top three floors of the structure collapsed into the basement. What was left of Mr. Molitor looked a lot like a blackened pipe cleaner."

Figueroa had been staring at the tabletop.

"Wait!" she said suddenly. She knew that wasn't the way to talk to the brass, and said in a quieter voice, "If you'll give me a minute, to go get something, I think I can explain what happened."

She got up.

Wardron said, "You can explain it right here."

"If I may leave for just a minute, sir, I can demonstrate."

"One minute, then."

Figueroa took two Styrofoam cups from the table that held the coffee urn and was back in less than a minute with two cups of water.

"Would you put the fingers of your left hand in one of these and the fingers of your right hand in the other, Deputy Wardron?"

"No. Explain to me what you think you're trying to do."

"Well maybe Commander Sazerac will, while I explain. We can always repeat it." Sazerac, intrigued, did as she said.

"One cup is hot water and one is cold. On the night of the fire, Officer Bennis had patted snow all over the brother, outdoors, and then ran back into the burning apartment. While he was doing that, I was pulling the woman out of the kitchen. She was hot to the touch and felt like she was starting to blister. When I came back, I felt along the hot wall. The instant Officer Bennis returned from outside, we both touched Mr. Molitor."

Commander Sazerac said, "I begin to see."

"Mr. Molitor was dead, but only ten to twenty minutes dead, so his skin was probably about the temperature of mine today. Commander, will you use both hands to touch my forearm?"

Sazerac did so. He smiled. "Amazing. Your arm feels warm to my right hand and cold to my left." Sazerac turned to Wardron. "The same arm," he said. "And it feels entirely different." He gestured to Wardron. "Want to try it?"

Figueroa and Bennis sat in their squad car. Bennis said, "Reminds me of this case I had once."

Figueroa sighed loudly, but Bennis knew she liked his stories.

"Guy decided to rob a fraternity house late at night, on a night when there had been a late snow. Flat, untouched snow leading up to the door. So he says to himself 'If I walk in backward, they'll think it was somebody from inside who stole the stuff, because there won't be any tracks leading in.' "

"Not a bad plan."

"Which he proceeds to accomplish. Picks up a lot of odds and ends, one or two wallets, a ten-inch TV, a boom box, and leaves. Kids get up in the morning, call the cops, we come in, see the tracks. Well, we'd been onto a guy in the neighborhood we knew'd been doing this kind of stuff. Go pick him up. Now he's got a problem. He wants to ask about tracks in the snow, but he shouldn't know anything about it, see?"

"Yup."

"So he says, real cute, 'You'd think you could tell whether it was an inside or outside job, snow like this and all.' "

"Real subtle."

"Yeah. Well, we said, 'We did and we knew by the tracks it was an outside job.' He says, all astounded, 'That's impossible! I faced backward, *going and coming both!*' "

Suze Figueroa giggled. "They get cute, but they never get smart."

"So you see, Figueroa, it's like this case with the fire. The way things are is all a matter of which angle you're looking at it from."

"Right, Bennis. Got it. Want to do a movie after work?"

He checked around to make sure nobody was watching and put his arm over her shoulders. "Let me take you to dinner, Figueroa. We missed Valentine's Day."

While doing research for "Hard Luck" and "Hard Women," I had been having a great time going on ride-alongs with cops and roll calls at Chicago Police stations. Cops see a completely different city from the rest of us, and they tell the best stories. I wanted to 'immortalize' some of my police officer friends. This is the first appearance of Norm Bennis and Suze Figueroa, two Chicago patrol cops. They did their detecting in several short stories and then went on to star in novels, including Killer.app, *and* Good Cop Bad Cop.

The Lower Wacker Hilton

"So, eight-fifteen A.M. we go screamin' in there," Officer Susannah Maria Figueroa said, "like it's a burglary in progress, and here's this guy—"

"Five foot zero," Norm Bennis said, "with four hairs on his head, all four of 'em combed across the top."

"Know the type," said Stanley Mileski, leaning back against his locker.

Figueroa pulled her walkie-talkie off the Velcro patch on her jacket and stuck it back on in a more comfortable position. "So it's eight-thirty give or take and he'd just got to the office, looked in the back room where the safe was, now he's hoppin' up and down on these *little* feet and yelping, like, saying 'It's gone! It's gone!' Pointin' through the door. Well, we go in and take a look and sure enough, the safe's gone. No doubt about it."

Norm Bennis said, "Big pale patch on the wall, clean patch on the floor."

"So he's jiggling and yelping and stuff, and he says, 'This safe's supposed to be burglar-proof, can't be jimmied, can't

51

be opened, can't be blasted, made right here in Chicago, they promised me it can't be opened, and *now look!*' and he puts these little tiny hands up to his face and he starts to cry."

Stanley "Lead Balls" Mileski said, "Jeez, I hate it when citizens do that."

Kim Duk O'Hara, their rookie, said, "Me too."

"So Norm here," Figueroa cocked her head toward her partner Bennis, who was a black man of medium height and *very* wide shoulders, now lounging back against the water fountain, "Norm says where in Chicago'd you buy it and the guy tells us. Norm says to the foot officer wait here and we go tearin' over to the safe company. Go in. There's the manager just unlockin' his office. Guy looks like Dwight Eisenhower, manages the Presidential Safe and Security Company."

Mileski said, "I ask you."

O'Hara said, "Who's Dwight Eisenhower?"

Bennis said, "He confirms. Safe can't be blasted, can't be opened without the combination, door's flush so you can't pry it. Set o' numbers on a horizontal dial, you have to slide 'em to the right combination. Can't hear any tumblers fall. Nothin'."

"So Norm says, here it's nine A.M., you just gettin' in? Manager says yeah. Bennis says, 'Your company name on the safe?' Manager says yeah. Bennis says, 'Can't be opened? I got an idea.' "

"Years of experience," Norm said, who was thirty-six to Figueroa's twenty-five.

"Phone rings. Bennis says 'May I?' and picks it up before Eisenhower even had a chance.

" 'Why, yes, sir,' Bennis is saying, nice as a cemetery plot salesman. 'We can help you with that. We'll come right on over.' Hangs up, says 'C'mon.'

"We slide on over to North Sedgwick, up the stairs, apart-

52

ment three-F, ring the bell, door opens, Bennis yells, 'Surprise!' We leap in, Bennis to the left, me to the right, I mean procedure was seriously followed here. And there's the safe and there's the perps."

"You coulda tied a ribbon on 'em," Bennis said.

"And there's the most humongous collection of crowbars and files and hammers and broken screwdrivers and crap you ever saw in your life."

Mileski was all bent over, laughing.

"Turned out," Figueroa said, "brother in law o' one o' the perps just won the lottery. Little lotto or some such. Won twelve thou. Here it is just before Christmas. Our perp was jealous. Wanted to do just as good for his family."

Norm Bennis stood upright, drew down his cheeks and eyelids and intoned, "Ah, yes. Jealousy is a dismal thing."

"Six fifty-nine and forty-seven seconds," Mileski said, looking at his watch. They all piled through the door into the rollcall room and sat down. As the digital clock on the wall changed to 7:00::00 he said, "Ding!"

Sergeant Touhy's face showed expression number four: Extreme Patience with the Behavior of Children.

"Settle down, troops, let's read some crimes."

The rollcall room at Chicago's First District station had its Christmas decorations up. Two loops of tinsel garlands over the door and a plastic wreath near the blackboard. The tinsel had shed as if it had mange and the bow on the wreath was sagging like a weeping willow.

"Figueroa," Bennis whispered, "this needs a woman's touch."

"Screw it, Bennis."

"Somebody to iron that bow, like."

Sergeant Touhy had a raft of pictures of shoplifters. "The stores are crowded. But some of these jerks are after big-

ticket items. They're your diamond, expensive-watch gen-
tlemen. You get a call and find the store detective got one o'
these babies, hold him."

"There's gotta be a million shoplifters in Chicago, Sarge,"
Mileski said.

"Hey, these got a history. *Career* shoplifters."

"But—"

"They're easy to prosecute, Mileski."

"But—"

"Mileski, you see somebody picking up a Honda under his
arm and taking it home, be my guest."

"But—"

"Mileski, these are the ones if we don't get 'em, we get
criticized, get my drift?" Touhy's voice was taking on a dangerous edge. "You want to bail out Lake Michigan with a
spoon, do it on your own time, okay?"

Mileski shut up.

"About yesterday, Bennis and Figueroa?"

"Yes, boss," they said in chorus.

"You were outta your district."

"Two blocks, Sarge," Bennis said.

"Districts is districts, Bennis. Plus you're supposed to
leave that crap to the detectives. What's the area commander
gonna think when he hears about this stunt of yours with the
safe?"

"That they saved some work?"

"Bennis! You're on the edge of a—"

"Gee, Sarge," Figueroa said. "Tell the commander we
were in hot pursuit."

"Shit!" Touhy slammed down the notebook. "Okay, you
clowns. Hit the bricks and clear."

Figueroa and Bennis were almost to the door when Touhy
yelled, "And don't do it again!"

★ ★ ★ ★ ★

Susannah Maria Figueroa was not in the best frame of mind today. She didn't really like working second watch. Third watch, three to eleven P.M. was better. Today she was missing her daughter Elena's first-grade holiday play. Elena was going to be half of a reindeer.

Suze Figueroa said, "I'll drive," and climbed into the car with Bennis. After a minute or two the seriously macho mars lights and all the seriously macho dash stuff had her feeling better. Like they always did.

The radio kicked in.

The dispatcher said, "One thirty-one."

"Thirty-one." It was Mileski's voice.

"See the woman at Chestnut and Michigan regarding found property."

"Michigan and Chestnut. Ten-four, squad."

"Thanks."

"Or was that Chestnut and Michigan?" Mileski said.

"Try Chestnut and Michigan and if she's not there try Michigan and Chestnut," the dispatcher said, laughing.

" 'Four."

"Someday he's going to go too far at the wrong moment," Bennis said. "With the wrong person."

The radio said, "One twenty-seven."

"Twenty-seven."

"Check the alley behind Clark Street in the four-hundred block. Supposed to be a nine-year-old kid driving a blue Oldsmobile. Citizen called it in."

"Ten-four."

The radio went on with its usual chatter. Bennis and Figueroa cruised their beat, admiring the Christmas lights.

"Cars going to the strongarm robbery at Eight-six-oh North Lake Shore take a disregard."

Silence for a few seconds.

"One twenty-two?"

"Twenty-two."

"Take an ag batt at Seven-one-seven North Rush. One twenty-three?"

"Twenty-three."

"Your VIN is coming back clear."

"Thanks, squad."

The radio said, "One thirty-three."

Bennis picked up and said, "Thirty-three."

"Complaint from a citizen, approximately Two-oh-oh South Wacker. Citizen says somebody's moanin' down in the sewer there."

"Name o' the citizen, squad?"

"Concerned's the name. Concerned Citizen. Not likely to be around when you get there."

"Ten-four, squad."

With the mike key closed, Bennis said, "Shit. Sewers."

Bennis and Figueroa rolled down Wacker, but they didn't see anything. There wasn't any citizen standing around wringing his hands in the two-hundred block. Since Figueroa was behind the wheel, Bennis got out on the sidewalk and stood listening. Figueroa saw him shiver a little.

"Jeez, that was eerie," he said, getting back in the car.

"What?"

"There's a kind of howlin' comin' outta that grate in the sidewalk."

"See anything?"

"Figueroa, my man, wouldn't I let you know if I did? Hang a left and let's get into Lower Wacker."

Two hundred years ago, the place where the center of Chicago now stands was a swamp. Some people think not much has changed.

When Chicago was a young frontier town, the swampy areas were mostly left as they were, filled with water and mud and garbage, and as the town grew, filled with the poor, living in tents and shacks. After the Great Chicago Fire, things were different.

There was big money in Chicago—lumber money, meat packing money, money from making harvesters and combines, money from the burgeoning railhead. Big money went into improving the city. The downtown streets were raised above the swamp or flood level. Whole areas of the Loop were built on iron stilts, the pavements were raised, and gradually the sidewalks were filled in and the vacant land stuffed with buildings until you could walk from one end of downtown to another and not realize it was underlain by swamp.

The only remnant of all this raising of the city was a series of secondary streets below the level where the sun shone. Some, like Lower Wacker, which runs under Wacker Drive along the Chicago River, are regularly used and are favorites of taxi drivers and city cognoscenti for getting places in a hurry.

Others are used primarily by loading trucks and delivery vans, picking up and delivering to the sub-basement levels of glitzy hotels and posh restaurants. Still others carry heat conduits, sewer mains, or parts of the underground transportation system.

Occasionally, one of the daylight-level streets will collapse without warning, leaving a hole at street level, a few cars in the muck at the bottom, pedestrians standing around on top gaping, and the rats underneath scurrying away. The last time this happened a passerby took one look at the hole, which was fifteen feet deep and forty across, and threw himself into it, hoping to collect big damages from the city. Bystanders saw him do it, however, and the ploy failed.

But many of the tunnels and leftovers under the city are unexplored and forgotten. There are homeless living there, and the Mud People. Down in these tunnels it is always dark. They are perfect places for people or deals that don't want to see the light of day.

Figueroa and Bennis slid into the downgrade and pulled up at a stop sign. "That way," Bennis said.

Dimly lit, Lower Wacker stretched away in both directions. They couldn't see any great distance because of the forest of support beams. Vertical iron beams ran down the pavement between the traffic lanes; cement pylons with iron cores held up the fifty-floor hotels that loomed unseen above them. Produce trucks roared out of the gloom from side alleys.

"Go about thirty yards," Bennis said.

Thirty yards in was a side alley. "Let's try this," he said.

"Yeah, it looks like real swell fun," Figueroa said.

The side alley was actually a tunnel, lit by very dim bulbs at hundred-yard distances. Most of it was sunk in gloom. Ahead the pavement was too narrow for the squad car.

Bennis started walking. Figueroa stayed ten seconds more to lock up the car. Leave one unlocked, come back and it's gone. Plus, God forbid you should leave the door open. Get rats in the car.

Figueroa caught up with Bennis and together they picked their way slowly along the tunnel, listening. The tunnel walls were concrete, striped vertically with a hundred years of ooze from the streets above. In some places stalactites of dried road salts and minerals and dirt depended from the pitted ceiling. Puddles of dank ooze lay in the low spots.

They turned down the sound on their radios. They had gone about forty or fifty feet when they heard a howl. For an instant—it sounded animal. Then it broke apart into sobs.

Figueroa and Bennis grimaced at each other, aware that they both had just resisted an urge to hold hands.

There was a still smaller side tunnel nearby. Inexplicably, two el tracks ran into this side tunnel on crossties and then ended, dead, having run twenty feet from nowhere to nowhere.

"Kelite?" Figueroa said, very softly.

But Bennis, thinking that a flashlight beam would only give warning that they were coming, shook his head.

The moaning increased.

In the cavern ahead was a dim glow, flickering yellowish on one side and bluish on the other. It outlined a group of figures so mingled in the dimness that Figueroa couldn't guess whether there were two or six. Over the figures loomed what looked like an ancient oak tree. The scene, Figueroa thought, was Druidic. She shivered.

As she and Bennis drew closer, the light seemed brighter. It came from two sources, a squat candle in an aluminum pie tin on the cement floor and indirect light on a part of the wall farther along that looked like it slanted in from an air shaft. The ancient tree became a heat duct that split into three arms near the top of the tunnel.

There was silence now ahead. The people had seen them. Bennis and Figueroa moved closed.

"Jeez," Figueroa whispered. "The Corrugated Cardboard school of interior decoration."

Between the heat duct, which was nearest them, and the airshaft, which was farthest away, were four areas against the wall. Figueroa thought of them as areas, because *rooms* was too strong a word and *beds* wasn't quite right, either. They were personal spaces, most separated by corrugated cardboard. The one nearest the heat duct was made from the top of a refrigerator or stove carton, laid on its side. Into this its owner had pushed a cracked piece of foam rubber pad, long enough to make a bed. The carton would enclose the upper half of a sleeper, for privacy. The space next to this was made of a big carton cut lengthwise. This formed a coffin-like bed and inside it were several layers of corrugated board, raising the bottom ten inches or so off the floor, away from the cold and damp. The other two, which were farther away, were also made of portions of corrugated board padded with many layers of newspaper.

In and around all of them were ripped scarves, dirty jackets, magazines, pieces of blankets, shoes, a pink bedsheet, Band-aid cans, soup cans, toilet paper, potato chip bags, duct tape, plastic bags, a saucepan, three or four lopsided pillows, a small pile of maybe half a dozen potatoes, several wine bottles, and a plastic-wrapped package of carrots.

On the pavement against the far wall was a tea kettle, a piece of bread, a small metal trash can, a circle of bricks with a lot of ashes and black coals in the middle, a can of charcoal lighter fluid, a can of Sterno, and a badly dented skillet.

Figueroa took all this in at a glance, at the same time keeping an eye on the human component of the scene.

Two men stood holding a third, who had been crying.

Figueroa said, "What seems to be the trouble here?"

They all stared at the two cops. Figueroa had the impression that a silent message of caution had gone out between them.

The smallest man, whose head jiggled on his neck said, "He's dead."

"Who's dead?" Bennis said.

"Chas. Chas. He's dead. He's dead." He was pointing, his finger trembling, toward the bed nearest the airshaft. It was so tumbled with clothing that they had not seen the body. "Dead, dead," he said, nodding over and over. The other men shifted their feet and waited.

"Stay here," Bennis said to the three men.

The job of the first uniforms on a scene is to check it out, see if a crime has been committed or if somebody is hurt. If somebody's hurt, call the EMTs. If there's a dead body, close down the scene and call the techs and the detectives.

Bennis went to the body and knelt down. Figueroa kept a watch on the other men.

"Dead?" she asked Bennis.

"Dead."

"Paramedics?"

"He's cooling off already. Dead a coupla hours, maybe."

When Bennis came back Figueroa went and looked at the body. There was no obvious sign of violence. No blood. No knife sticking out. Just a gaping mouth, unshaven chin, and staring, clouded eyes.

Figueroa said to the three men, "Can I see your driver's licenses?"

The man who had been crying giggled briefly. "Don't have any."

"Why not?"

"Got rolled. Inna shelter."

"I have one," the oldest of the three said. Bennis turned to the others and said, "Names?"

Willie Sims was a smallish black man of indeterminate age with white whisker stubble and a coating of dust that made him look gray. Samo Marks was a smaller white man with dark whisker stubble and a layer of dirt that made him look gray. His head twitched, and when Bennis made a note of his name in his notebook he also made the comment "Addled."

The third man was slightly cleaner. Louis Papadopolous, who had a driver's license, had washed sometime in the last few days.

Samo hadn't washed recently, but the tears had flowed so freely down his cheeks that most of the lower part of his face was clean, if streaky. Even around his eyebrows, across which he had apparently swiped his sleeve, there was a clean patch.

"Occupation?" Bennis asked, in a tone of voice that suggested he was required to ask it, but thought it was stupid in this case.

Willie Sims shrugged, "I owned a restaurant. Had a fire. No insurance."

Samo Marks said, "Nothin,' nothin' a-tall." He waved his head back and forth. "Useta set pins," he said. "Bowling alley."

Papadopolous nodded at Samo as if he were doing very well. "They automated," Papadopolous said.

"And what about you, sir?" Figueroa asked, using her be-nice-to-the-public voice.

Papadopolous said, "Ad exec. We had a few—mm—deep cutbacks."

"Oh."

"I got into the sauce. Not any more." Figueroa gestured at the wine bottles. Papadopolous said, "Samo drinks, some. Chas too."

"Chas was zonked last night," Willie said.

"Zonked! Wasted!" Samo said.

"He 'as real nice, Chas, he 'as real nice," Samo said over and over. "Never hurt anybody." He started moaning again. *Emotionally labile,* Figueroa said to herself, having just spent four Thursday evenings in Supplemental Sensitivity Training.

"Useta lie there, look up the air shaft and tell us what went by," Willie said. "Mornings, people on their way to work. Like, just before we'd go to sleep."

"Yeah?"

Samo said, "Tell us all about the legsa the girls on the sidewalk up there. You know."

"Um, legs."

"Yeah, and some of 'em wouldn't be wearing any underwear. Sheet, you shoulda heard some a what he saw—" He stopped, abruptly realizing he was talking to a female-type officer. "Um, yeah, like shoes," he ended up.

"Well, sure."

"Kept us entertained," Papadopolous said.

"No TV here, ya see," Willie said.

"Who sleeps where?" she asked.

"Thas me." Willie said, with some pride, pointing at the piece of foam rubber near the heat duct.

"You got the choice place," Bennis said to Willie.

"Yeah. Nice and warm."

"That's me," Papadopolous gestured at the spot next to Willie, the layers of cardboard.

Samo said, "Over there," pointing to the pile of newspaper and tattered blankets that lay next to the dead Chas. All the while, Samo was moving his head back and forth, as if listening to music.

Chas's bed was a hodgepodge heap of old clothes, including a couple of stocking caps and a shoe. There was a torn plaid scarf over his lower body, though, and while it was a mess, neither that nor any of the bedding looked like it had been kicked around.

"He been sick?" Bennis asked.

"No, just the sauce."

"Well, we'll get the experts on it." Bennis grabbed his radio.

To Figueroa, watching, it looked for an instant like Papadopolous was either going to hit Bennis or run. Her hand moved an inch toward her sidearm.

63

"One thirty-three," Bennis said. "We've got a downer."

The radio said, "Bagzzt-*skeek*-urty-three."

"One thirty-three."

"Pzzzzmmmmm."

To Figueroa, Bennis said, "Shit. Reception's cruddy down here." Again he said, "One thirty-three."

Clear as day the radio said, "Thirty-three. You're not makin' it with your radio, sir. Borquat-muzzzz. Pip."

"Oh, excellent, swell, really sweet. I'd better go up the street and put out the word." He gave Figueroa a glance they'd exchanged maybe five hundred times, him to her or her to him. It meant, "You okay with this?"

She nodded.

"Back in two seconds."

Figueroa believed that Papadopolous's fear had less to do with Chas's actual death and more to do with the possibility that the police would arrest them or move them along to some less desirable place.

"Pretty sheltered here," she said, hoping he'd talk about it.

"We fixed Thanksgiving dinner in that," Papadopolous said, pointing to the small garbage can.

"Store give us a lil' turkey," Samo said.

"You roasted a turkey! In that?"

Papadopolous said, "We made a bed of charcoal briquets and put the can on top." He grinned at her, knowing she was finding it hard to believe they weren't all incompetent morons. "Shucks," he said, laying it on, "anybody'd been a Boy Scout could do it."

"Stores throw out stuff, it doesn't look fresh anymore," Willie said. "Vegetables, like. Pastry."

"How long you been living here?"

"How long?" Willie echoed. "Maybe since November?"

He looked at Papadopolous, who said, "November tenth we came here. The police drove us out of O'Hare."

"O'Hare, yeah," Samo said. "Druve us out."

Willie cackled. "They're bundling us into these buses. So they say, all horrified: 'Do you want O'Hare to look like *New York?*'"

"Took us a while to find this place," Papadopolous said, obviously uneasy, still thinking they were going to be moved along.

"This is a good place," Samo said, head nodding.

"Yeah, sweet," Willie said, chuckling again. "We call it the Lower Wacker Hilton."

"What do you do all day?"

They were all averting their eyes from the corpse.

"Well, day, see, we don't do anything, days," Willie said.

Samo said, "We sleep."

"Stores and all those fancy restaurants, they don't want us millin' around, see?" Willie said. "In daylight."

"They don't mind so much at night," Papadopolous said. "So we get back here just before dawn, go to bed. Get our healthful eight hours. This time of year it's not light until seven, seven-thirty anyhow. Sleep to four-thirty. It's dark at four-thirty, so we get up and go to work. Works out real neat."

Willie chuckled. "Yeah, out there movin' and shakin'."

"Dumpsters!" Samo said brightly. "Garbage cans!"

Papadopolous said, "They don't mind too much as long as you don't throw stuff all over the street."

Samo suddenly broke out, "You oughta see some guys they just dump over a can, throw everything, throw shit all over the sidewalk. We allus been real careful." He grabbed a quick glance at the corpse of Chas and started to snuffle.

Willie said, "Some folks make a bad name for honest street people."

"Basically you're scavengers, then," Figueroa said to Willie.

"Scavengers? No, I don't think we're scavengers."

"What are you?"

"Beachcombers," Willie Sims said.

Bennis came back. Figueroa raised her eyebrows at him. He said, "They will be with us, my man, as soon as is consistent with the pursuit of their other duties."

"Gawd!" Figueroa said.

Figueroa caught sight of two eyes glowing in the darkness behind the heat duct. She jumped but covered it by pretending to turn to get a better view.

"Aw, gee," Samo said, seeing what it was.

Papadopolous made a clucking sound.

An animal stepped out of the shadows.

"Jeez, a cat!" Figueroa said.

Papadopolous said, "We feed him. Bring something back for him every night. When we can. Keep him around as much as possible."

"Why?"

"For the mice. And the rats."

"Rats!" Samo shrieked. "Get yer toes."

"Not yours!" Willie said scornfully. Samo's feet were extremely dirty.

Figueroa said, "We got rats down here the size of Toyotas. No cat can deal with Chicago tunnel rats. These rats scare cats outta seven lives."

"Not this one."

It stalked farther forward.

The cat was a marmalade tom with a huge ruff. He had a round face that looked more like bobcat than tomcat and his body was a barrel.

"Weighs thirty-five pounds," Papadopolous said.

"Yeah, okay," Figueroa said. "I guess rats wouldn't scare him."

"Name's Adolf."

There was the sound of heavy feet in the distance, getting closer.

Suddenly Samo started crying. "He kilt'm."

"Killed who?"

"Chas. Smothered'm. Adolf smothered'm. Slept on his face and smothered'm."

"Okay," said Figueroa, "that's enough."

She turned and took Samo's arm.

"Look," she said, "the court's probably gonna say you're not really responsible." Willie and Papadopolous were staring at her as if she was nuts. "You've been drinking crap. You got a can of Sterno over there and a piece of bread to strain it through. You were depressed. You didn't have any-thing in this world. You wanted something. Any one thing of your own. And you went out of your head. You smothered Chas with your pillow."

"Nooooo—"

"Figured Papadopolous'd help move him, lose the body, rather than have your space here get discovered."

"Nooooo—"

"Come and look up here."

Figueroa dragged Samo over the airshaft. They looked up. There was a vertical cement shaft with light at the top, light coming through opaque glass disks set in an iron grid. There was nothing else to see. Absolutely nothing.

Samo shrieked.

"How'd you know, Figueroa?" Bennis said.

"Brilliance."

"C'mon, my man. This is me you're talkin' to."

"Cats don't smother people, Bennis. Useta say they smothered babies, but they don't."

"So the guy was wrong. Chas could of died of natural causes."

"Then why'd he think up an explanation for Chas being smothered? Huh?"

"Beats me."

"Who benefited from Chas's death? What did they have of value, any of them? Two things. The heat pipe and the view from the air shaft. Willie and Chas. They had the prizes."

"Yeah."

"See, they always lie low in the daylight. None of 'em ever had a chance to look up the airshaft. That was Chas's spot. They got back before daylight and everybody had his own space. None of 'em had ever looked up the airshaft, so they didn't know there was nothing to see. They didn't know that Chas was just entertainin' 'em."

"And when Samo realized —"

"I think he was already feeling remorse. When he realized, that was when he really broke."

"Well, I'll tell you what *I* think, Figueroa. I think you go on workin' at this, my man, you gonna get real good at your job."

I love bookstores. Agatha Christie loved the library as a place for murder, maybe because it contrasted so well with violence. One of her mysteries was "The Body in the Library." These days, most houses aren't big enough to have a separate room for a library, but we all have and enjoy the neighborhood bookstore. It seems to me that if you know bookstores well enough, you might be able to solve a crime committed there . . .

Shelved

My name is Susannah Maria Figueroa. At ten-thirty on a cold but sharply bright spring morning in Chicago, I was riding alone in car 1-27, because my usual partner, Officer Norm Bennis, was out with an injury. Not an IOD, injured on duty. He claimed he had been trying to get out a *Terminator* tape that was stuck in his VCR and Arnold Schwarzenegger had attacked and mutilated his hand. Bennis's fingertips were definitely mangled. But Bennis is so fickle in his romantic life that I have learned not to inquire too closely when bizarre accidents happen to him.

At any rate, I was on second watch, which is seven A.M. to three P.M., and I called in on the radio.

"One-twenty-seven."

The dispatcher said, "Go ahead, twenty-seven."

"Could I get early lunch?"

"Sure. Where you gonna be?"

"Bookworm on Michigan."

"Bookworm? Doesn't sound like a lunch counter to me."

"Trust me. To me it's lunch."

"Ten-four, twenty-seven."

I responded, "Ten ninety-nine." Ninety-nine means I'm a

one-person unit. Two-person units say "Ten-four." Ten-four units are more likely to get sent to gang wars and men armed with Uzis holed up in alleys. Still, I'd rather have Bennis back and be a ten-four unit.

Bennis was the reason I was going to skip lunch and go to the Bookworm. Friday would be Bennis's anniversary. Ten years in the department. This was a very big deal, and I wanted to buy him something nice. But he's hard to shop for.

I'd racked my brains for a week—rhinestone handcuffs? A tweed wool deerstalker? A bottle of rye for his bottom drawer? A suede case with silver monogram for his walkie-talkie? And I finally thought of something. There was a history of the Peelers, the Irish constabulary founded in 1812 by Robert Peel. The Peelers are considered the first real police force.

So I parked and went into the Bookworm to shop.

The Bookworm contains three floors of floor-to-ceiling books. You can take a book down from a shelf and sit in one of the armchairs strategically scattered through the sales space, leaf through your book and see if you want to buy it. There are even shelves along the stairs, so as you walk up to the second and third floors, you run your eye along title after title. Yum!

And they have salespeople who *read!* When I asked for a book on Peelers, they wouldn't send me to cookbooks.

"I'm looking for a history of the Peelers," I said to a thirtyish man who stood next to a display of dictionaries—French/English, English/French, German, Polish, Dutch, Japanese, Hungarian, Navajo—

"Oh, yes. It's in History—in the back on the left, over there." He pointed. "If you'll just ask Sonia, she's our history specialist. I'm the reference specialist."

Sonia proved to be a thin woman of about twenty-five with

long, lank black hair and a long, black, tubelike dress. She knew exactly what I wanted, even though I didn't know the author's name.

"That book's been doing pretty well," she said.

"I wouldn't think history would just jump off the shelves."

She laughed and waved an arm. "Look at these. This is our Kennedy section. Nine out of ten of those *do* jump off the shelves."

"How come the other ten percent don't?"

"Beats me. Some years the Civil War is hot. Some years it isn't. Some years it's the American Revolution. I wish you could tell me why."

From there I wandered into Reference.

The young man who had directed me to History said, "Can I help you?" His name tag told me he was Eric.

"Oh, just looking, thanks." I fingered a book on plant poisons. They had several copies. "Do a lot of people want to poison somebody?" I asked.

"Must be." He gave a shy smile. "We've sold quite a lot of them."

"That's unnerving. Well, thanks."

I browsed. What a nice word, browse. I picked up books and put them down, and somehow, two that I hadn't intended to buy managed to stick to me.

On my way toward the front I was waylaid by the mystery wing, which was in the right rear of the store, opposite the history area. A new novel by Carolyn Hart leaped into my hand, and I sat down in an armchair to read for just a minute. The Mystery salesperson, with a name tag that read "Jane," sailed near, pushing a wheeled cart with hundreds of paperbacks on it. She said cheerily to me, "Oh, that one's been very popular!" and passed by. Jane was pretty, big blue eyes, large hips, large bosom, small waist, bouncy blond hair.

Dimly, I was aware of some cheerful voices in the background, and my police radio stuttered and squawked now and then. But what was that to me? I was reading! Then I was aware of some irritable voices in the background. Not my problem. I was reading!

When I was a child, we lived in a house with an attic. There was something strange about the attic. It was all bare golden wood, and the sun came through a dusty, narrow little window. The light was amber, and it was warm and dry up there, with dust motes moving sleepily in the air. I could take a book up with me and start to read, and suddenly four or five hours had passed and I never noticed.

Bookstores affect me that way. I'll go in to buy exactly one item, and suddenly it's an hour later.

I jumped up at some really loud voices, and realized that I was going to run over my lunch period. That could be very bad! The CPD is like the Army: you're supposed to be where you're supposed to be when you're supposed to be there, and no yuppie-type arguments about lack of motivation.

I race-walked to the nearest cash register, which was in the mystery department. But there was no one there to check me out. I heard excited talking from farther to the front of the store and went there.

Six salespeople, including Sonia, Jane, and Eric, clustered around the front. Near them a man in a dark suit, labeled Gerald Johnstone, Manager, was just putting down the phone. Of the six salespeople, five were talking. The manager, Johnstone, said, "They're going to send somebody."

"I should've stayed there," one of the salespeople moaned. His name tag said "Mark."

"It's not your fault."

"This is just so—"

"Ohmigod!"

"In a bookstore! How could they take advantage—"

Sonia laughed wryly. "It's not any more *moral* to rob a shoe store! Or a drugstore!"

"What I meant—"

I said, "What's going on?"

Most of them looked at me as if it was no business or mine—and why should they think differently, since they didn't know I was a cop?—but Jane disgustedly said, "Teenagers!"

At that instant my radio spoke. "One thirty-three."

Another voice answered, "Thirty-three." It was my buddy, Stanley Mileski.

"Thirty-three, I have a robbery at 213 North Michigan."

I punched my radio. "Twenty-seven."

"Twenty-seven, go."

"Is that the Bookworm, squad? Because I'm there."

"Whoever called it in didn't give 911 the name or the store. They apparently hung up too soon." Behind Eric, Mr. Johnstone began to blush. So he was more flustered than he seemed.

"That's this address, isn't it, Mr. Johnstone?" I asked him.

"Yes, it is."

"I'm here, squad. I'll take care of it."

"Sure thing, one twenty-seven. Weren't you supposed to be back from lunch?"

"I was about to clear when I noticed the disturbance." Well, it was only half a lie. I'd been vaguely aware of the disturbance; but I'd been reading.

All right, I was more than a little annoyed with myself. Apparently I'd allowed a burglary to happen right under my nose. Susannah Maria Figueroa, fearless law enforcement person and noted screw-up.

I now had six salespeople plus Mr. Johnstone to deal with.

The three I hadn't met were named Debbie, Mark, and Mike. All were under thirty-five. Debbie was a slight, attractive woman with chestnut hair cut short. Mark was solidly built, a hockey-player type with crinkly dark hair. Mike was tall and slender and blond. Don't any nice grandmotherly women with white hair ever get hired by bookstores anymore?

"Tell me what happened."

Johnstone, to make up for his dropping the stitch in talking with 911, was clear and unemotional. "About twenty minutes ago a big group of teenagers, well, twelve to fourteen years old, came into the store—"

"Seven teenagers altogether," Sonia said firmly. Johnstone slid his eyes at her sideways. I wondered how long Sonia would go on working here.

"Possibly seven, and they started running around the store, horsing around, picking up books, giggling at covers . . ." As he said this he was standing near a cover showing a naked woman standing on a giant pineapple. I looked at it, and he looked to where I was looking. We both turned our heads back. "They were distracting everybody."

"And . . ." I encouraged him.

"Ahh . . ." he sighed. "They were all over this floor, and I'm afraid the staff left their cash registers to try and round up the kids."

"They were wrinkling the dustcovers!" Jane said.

"And finger-marking them," Debbie said. "These matte-finish dustcovers, even if you wipe them with a soft cloth, you can't get the finger marks off."

Sonia added, "We weren't just leaving our *posts*. We were protecting stock!"

"Anyway, after they decided they didn't want to buy anything, and left, Mark here—Mark is Mainstream Fiction—Mark here went to his cash register to ring up a sale, and there was no cash in it."

"Some coins," Mark said. "No paper money."

"How much do you think you had?"

"About three hundred and fifty dollars. Could have been four hundred." He almost, but not quite, started to wring his hands. "I should have stayed at the register."

"Never mind that. Was it in small bills? Large bills?"

"Mostly ones, fives, and twenties."

"All right. Now, all of you tell me—where did they go and where did they *not* go?"

"Oh, I just don't know," Jane said. "Everyplace."

Sonia said, "Just *this* floor. They didn't go upstairs."

Sonia was emerging as a person of considerable alertness.

Johnstone said, "It's a known technique of thieves, isn't it? Create a diversion and empty a cash register?"

"Yes. It happens."

They stood about, gaping at me. I said, "Show me the register."

It was the one in Mainstream Fiction, of course. Sure enough, there was no paper money in it. "Don't touch it," I said. "I'll call the evidence techs."

Debbie said, "Fingerprints?"

Michael said, "Mmmm!"

"While this was going on, did any salespeople come down from upstairs?"

"No. They're not supposed to. There aren't as many of them upstairs and you can't leave the stock alone. We have a lot of shoplifting."

"Especially tapes and computer stuff from Three," Sonia said.

"Two is Music and Video," Debbie said helpfully.

Sonia added, "I think I would have noticed if any salespeople had come down the stairs."

I thought she would, too. "Good. So the upstairs people won't be able to tell me anything. Can you have one of them come down and run the front cash registers while we talk?"

Johnstone got on the intercom and called upstairs.

I went on, "Did all of you leave your posts?"

They squirmed, but the answer was that yes, they all did. They were running around shooing kids.

Mark said, "Nasty children."

Mike said, "And they had on these hideously bright clothes."

My niece favors lime-green worn with orange and electric-blue, but I wasn't here to argue.

"Did you see anything in their hands when they left?"

"I'm afraid we were just so glad that they *were* leaving . . ." Johnstone said. He let the sentence die there.

Sonia said, "No. I don't think they were carrying anything."

"But it could have been hidden under their clothes," Jane said.

"Did any customers come down from upstairs?"

"Not while the teenagers were here."

"It wasn't long," Mark added. "I mean, altogether they were in and out in less than five minutes."

Johnstone said, "And morning isn't our busiest time or day. It will be soon, though," he added nervously, looking at his watch, then at the front door. "Lots of people shop here on their lunch hour."

Sonia was more alert to the direction of my questions. "Why are you asking?"

"Well, obviously, the teenagers aren't the only people who could have taken the money."

"There weren't all that many other customers here," Johnstone said.

"But there were the seven of you."

"What? We didn't take it!"

"Has this ever happened before, Mr. Johnstone?"

"Cash register thefts? Maybe a couple of times. Shoplifting is more common, though—"

"I mean exactly this kind of thing. Cash registers rifled while there was a disturbance in the store."

"Ahh . . ."

Sonia helped again. "About a month ago. There was a bunch of football player types in here with loud radios. And a few weeks before that we had a woman faint dead away in the store and the man with her totally freaked." There was something in Sonia's tone. Could it be suspicion? She added, "We don't get very many people making disturbances in here."

"Did you call the police both times?"

"Yes. But they never found the thieves. Or the money."

Mark said, "But it *is* a known theft technique?"

I said, "Yes, and it's a great opportunity for the staff, too. I'm sorry, but what I need to do is look in everybody's locker. Also, three hundred and fifty dollars in mostly smallish bills is too much to hide on your person very easily unless you're wearing outdoor clothes, but I want the women to pat each other down and the men to do the same just to be sure."

"You can't make me do this," Debbie said.

Johnstone took this opportunity to get decisive, and I'm glad he did, because I'd have had a hard time carrying through. If people don't voluntarily agree, a police officer has to jump through hoops sometimes. Johnstone said, "I want everybody to be calm and cooperative about this. I'm sure we're all perfectly innocent, and this is the quickest way to prove it."

Nobody was wearing voluminous multilayered clothing, so they were done with the search in minutes. Then we trooped to the lockers in the back room. It looked like I was going to move around guided by a crowd of seven wherever I went in the store.

The lockers were in back, twenty-five of them. They were the metal kind like you have in high schools, and each employee had a combination lock.

"Which of you were here all three times the robberies happened?" I asked while I rummaged.

A chorus:

"I don't know . . ."

"Um, I was here . . ."

"All of us, I guess."

"I think I was . . ."

Sonia spoke up. "All of us salespeople were here. Mr. Johnstone was away at the ad agency the second time it happened."

There was a lot of stuff in the lockers. There were headache remedies: Anacin, aspirin, Tylenol. There were a couple of bottles of Pepto Bismol. Rubber bands, a Bible, paper clips, lots of knitted stocking caps and extra gloves, this being spring in Chicago. Several bottles of sunscreen in all ranges of "protection," also because of spring in Chicago. Scarves, boots, extra jackets, extra skirts, extra pants, a pressed shirt or two, dark glasses, candy bars, a pear, three apples, and several sandwiches, including a particularly revolting-looking banana and peanut butter on rye. There was one pack of cigarettes. It turned out Sonia smoked.

There was even money. Jane had a small plastic cup of coins. "For the bus," she said.

Mark had a twenty-dollar bill in a shoe. "Just in case."

"In case of what?" Sonia asked.

"In case of needing money."

But there was no stolen cash in any of the lockers.

"Where else could money be hidden?" I asked Johnstone.

"I don't know. Nowhere."

"The carpet's tacked down. The chairs don't have cushions."

"It wouldn't be—"

I said, "Wait. How about on a shelf? Behind some books?"

"Impossible!" he said.

"Why? Our crook could just stick the money behind some books and pick it up at the end of the shift, after the cops have left."

Jane said, "But this is the very beginning of the shift! The money would have to stay there all day. None of us gets to leave until five P.M. Any customer could come along any time all day and buy a book and find the money. It just wouldn't work."

"Except . . ." I said.

They all stared at me—Sonia, Johnstone, Jane, Eric, Mike, Mark, and Debbie.

"Except in their own department. Their own section. Every one of these specialists knows which books jump off the shelves and which sit there month after month after month."

"And that means . . ." Johnstone said, an idea beginning to dawn on him.

"It means when you find the money, you'll also know who put it there."

"It'll take forever to look behind all the books," he started to say, but I didn't answer. I had turned to Jane, who was weeping.

"I needed it. I really, really *needed* it." Her big blue eyes were drowned in tears.

"So you decided to blame your thefts on people you figured would easily look guilty?"

"I didn't mean it that way. I just needed the money so *bad!*"

I called for the evidence tech. Backup prints wouldn't hurt in case Jane changed her mind and decided she'd been beaten into confessing.

Johnstone wanted to give me the books I was buying, but I couldn't let him do that. By twelve the noon rush was starting and I was just about out of there. We found the money behind some Arsene Lupin reprints. I guess this shows Jane really knew her department—Lupin doesn't jump off the shelves the way Susan Dunlap and Margaret Maron do. Also Lupin is one of the few mystery heroes who doesn't solve murders. A thief turned detective, he solves thefts.

When I was a child, all the movies I saw that took place on water were set either on the Atlantic or Pacific Ocean. Lake Michigan is more changeable, more moody, and like Chicago, a real character. The Great Lakes area is the hardest place on earth to predict the weather. There are the extremes of subzero winters to heat wave summers, but no two days on the lake are the same, either.

Soon to Be

a Minor Motion Picture

It was the hand of Lady Luck, I suppose, that led me to watch the television news just before we found the actor and the one-man film crew. But I like to think Norm Bennis and I would have seen through their story anyway.

My name is Susannah Figueroa and I'm a Chicago Police officer.

My partner Norman Bennis said, "Is this living?"

"This is living!" I said.

"I mean, this *is* living!"

"You can say that again."

The sun struck glints from the waters of Lake Michigan. A warm hint of breeze caressed my face as I sat in the open cabin. Our small boat, its motor off, rose slowly and lowered almost imperceptibly on a glassy calm sea. "Like being rocked in the arms of Morpheus," said Bennis, who was in back at the helm, ostensibly observing. I could see that his eyelids hung lower than a furled mainsail.

"I didn't know you could wax poetic," I said.

"Hey! That's the way I wax when I wax."

I was eating my lunch at the table in the tiny cabin of the Chicago Police Department Marine Unit powerboat. We had

81

decided that I would eat while Bennis stayed at the wheel, then vice versa. As I watched, a wave thrown up in the wake of a passing water-skier slapped the boat and tossed a few drops of spray onto my partner. He didn't move.

If we had been on patrol in the city, the only spray would have been from the spitting of air conditioners in high-rises. The breeze would be automobile exhaust funneled down urban canyons over superheated road tar. The only rocking would take place as our squad car bumped into potholes.

The CPD goes through off and on stages in its use of the Marine Patrol. More than once the unit had been cut out of the budget entirely, the City Council having decided it was too expensive. Then somebody would drown or a tour boat would capsize and the next day they'd have a Marine Unit patrol again.

Bennis and I were not regular Marine Unit officers. I had put in two months on it early in my training. And Bennis, who is ten years older than I am, had been in the Navy and had spent one year in the Marine Unit back in 1987. We'd been roped into duty this week in late August because of an unfortunate accident.

Some genius at the central cop shop had decided that the least expensive way to fuel the Marine Unit humans was to have sandwiches made downtown for their lunches and put aboard in a cooler. Somebody had neglected to keep them cool enough before they were put into the cooler. Salmonella can take twelve to twenty-four hours to develop, so before anybody realized what was happening, everybody had eaten the sandwiches. Seventy percent of the Marine Unit staff was now hors de combat. All experienced personnel and all half-experienced personnel were being called in to take up the slack. We'd got the call at the crack of dawn: report to the dock.

This was fine with me and Bennis. We like each other, we're longtime squad car partners, and we thought a few days on a boat would be a splendid vacation. Our first really plum assignment in ages, in fact.

Bennis leaned back and said dreamily, "Figueroa, my man, I had this case a few years ago."

I knew I was about to be instructed in some point of policing. "Yes, Norm?"

"This guy—you know how Stibich always says the average crook is terminally stupid—this guy decides to rob a bank. But he's too lazy to scope it out ahead, see?"

"I know the type," I said.

"He figures he can just go in and muscle it. Takes his .38 and his seriously dangerous-looking black pants and black shirt with the cutout sleeves that show his delts and biceps and figures that's good enough to scare the piss out of any teller."

"Which it probably is."

"Oh, no doubt. Scares *me*. The gun anyhow. But see, he forgot one thing. He's got the bank all picked out. He's been passing by the building for years. One of those big banks made out of red polished granite, with the name carved across the front and big granite pillars and carved acanthus leaves—"

"Acanthus leaves! I didn't know you were so erudite, Bennis."

"Yes, you did. Probably a Louis Sullivan—"

"Who is Louis Sullivan?"

"A major architect of the early twenties, Suze, my man. I'm astonished you didn't know. Designed banks all over the place. Also the Chicago Opera House. And Carson Pirie Scott. And many more architectural triumphs."

"My, my!"

"In any case, a big bank. Impressive. Big steps leading up to the front doors. You know the kind of step that's so wide you have to take two steps on it?"

"Yeah. Not user-friendly."

"But stately. So he stashes his gun in his pocket and goes in. But unknown to him, the bank moved out years ago and the building has been taken over by a firm of lawyers. There's a big sign in one window, all gold letters, perfectly clear, but our guy doesn't bother to read it. In he goes. Doesn't even notice that the tellers' cages are gone. He marches up to a receptionist behind a mahogany desk at the back and says, 'Gimme all your money.'

"She says, 'I don't have any money. What do you think this is, a bank?'

"So he looks around now, and by that time one of the lawyers is coming over to the desk. He says, 'What's the trouble?'

"The secretary says, 'This man wants to rob us.'

"The lawyer says, 'This is a law office, young man.'

"By now our perp is mad, and he says, 'I don't care if this is a bank or an office, get all your money together and put it in a bag.'

"So they get some money out of wallets and purses and stick it in a paper bag, but the lawyer says to the guy, 'Okay. But you know I'm gonna have to charge you for this.'

"Perp says, 'What?'

"The lawyer says, 'I get $200 an hour and I'm gonna have to charge you for my time.'

"Perp looks at him, blinks, and says, 'Oh, hell! Forget it then!' and he throws the money bag at the lawyer and runs out the door."

I laughed so hard I spilled my Coke on the bench seat and had to wipe it up. It's very important to stay shipshape on a boat.

Bennis said, "And the moral of the story, Figueroa my man, is that they always do *something* stupid. In some cases you gotta look for it, but they always do something stupid."

I watched the noon news on a television set about the size of a large grape. There was some doubt about whether Chicago schools would open next week as they were scheduled to do. Apparently the teachers and the board had not yet agreed to come to the bargaining table.

Newscaster Bob Cole reported that there had been a morning rush hour pileup on the Edens Expressway. Finally he turned to his coanchor.

"Now, Heidi Amurao has the entertainment news," he said. "Heidi?"

"Thanks, Bob. Tonight is your last chance to see Frank Sinatra in concert. He's giving his farewell performance, 'My Kind of Town' at the old Chicago Theater. Tickets are said to be scarce. And Emeraude is in town. She's finishing filming of the major motion picture *Maid Marian* directed by Steven Lagerfeld in which she costars with Collum Greene. Emeraude, known for her austere profile and cool-cool-cool air on-screen, has finally agreed to film a torrid nude love scene for the picture. Rumors are that the segment is being filmed in deep secret somewhere on Lake Michigan. And in a surprise development, a reliable source states that despite earlier announcements, Emeraude is going to pull out of the forthcoming Lagerfeld remake of *Dark Passage* starring Collum Greene. Our source cites artistic differences that cropped up during the filming of *Marian*. On the music front, the search goes on for a new conductor for the Chicago Symphony Orchestra—"

Bennis said, "Emeraude? Nude? Where, where? WHERE?" and leaped up on the rail, balancing precariously and scanning the horizon with his hand shading his eyes.

"Please! Spare me. And besides, if you fall in, I won't fish you out." He stayed on the rail. "You know, that's odd about *Dark Passage*. The *Enquirer* said it was a done deal."

"She shouldn't have let that leak while she was still making this picture." He jumped back down.

"I don't think she let it, Bennis. I've heard Emeraude and her current guy Mitchen are fighting. She hit him with a pineapple from the centerpiece at a dinner last week. He probably ran to the gossipmongers with something she'd told him in confidence."

"Ah, pillow talk. Always very foolish."

I folded up my sandwich paper and lobbed it into a trash can. "Well, she changes men every three weeks whether they're used up or not. She used to be an item with Lagerfeld, and Collum before that."

"Fickle."

"Speaking of fickle, how's Annabella?"

"Annabella's history. I'm dating this Felicia now. She really is the one, Figueroa."

"We'll see about that."

Bennis went to the table to eat and I took his place at the helm. I noticed the start of a sunburn on my arm. Not bad, though. If we were out again tomorrow, I'd have to bring sunscreen. Still—thank goodness we got to wear short sleeves. A full uniform out here would be deadly.

When Bennis had finished lunch, we tooled around some more, first up toward Belmont Harbor, then down past the Planetarium. Since it was Thursday, not a weekend, and since Labor Day was still a week away, there were one or two boats visible, but not the armada that would be out on Saturday.

"My favorite," Bennis said, "is when we get boats as far as the eye can see and then some guy trails a water-skier down the middle, right in front of cigarette boats going at top speed."

"Top speed and drunk," I said.

Half a lazy hour later we issued a citation to one motor-boat operator who was laying down a serpentine track on the calm water.

"Fueled by gasoline and vodka," Bennis said.

Then, with not much going on, we ran farther out into Lake Michigan and stood half a mile offshore with the engine off, surveying the city. That was when we heard screaming.

We looked around, not seeing where it was coming from, and I actually stared down into the water. Then Bennis's eye picked up a motorboat coming toward us. Somebody on deck was waving.

As it got closer, I said, "Speak of the devil!"

It was Steven Lagerfeld and Collum Greene. What they were screaming was, "Help us! Emeraude's drowning!"

I stood on the deck of their twenty-five-foot cabin cruiser. I almost said, "Gee, you look just like in the movies," but that would have been naive and also trite, and a Chicago cop can't act that way. Collum Greene did look just like in the movies. He was the "new" style of hunk, red-haired, white freckled skin, although his nose and forearms were looking sunburned now, probably having exhausted the protection of his sunscreen. Collum's appeal was said to be of the boy-next-door sort. There had been nobody next door to me like that, unfortunately.

Lagerfeld was bony, swarthy, and dark-haired. He was more like the mugger next door.

Both men were extremely upset as we stood there on the deck in the sun. It was a warm day, and Collum was wearing a short-sleeve terry-cloth shirt over a skimpy bathing suit. His hair was wet and he was shivering. Lagerfeld was beautifully dressed in while linen pants and a cotton shirt, but he was shaking too.

"She fell overboard," Collum repeated several times. He kept grabbing at my hand when he said it. Bennis, in our boat, was on the radio, giving our position to the dispatcher to relay to the Coast Guard. At Meigs Field, which jutted out into Lake Michigan only a mile or so away, there was a rescue helicopter already taking off.

After Lagerfeld and Greene flagged us down, we had motored together to where they thought the movie star had gone into the water. But there was no sign of her. Behind us Chicago was almost out of sight in the haze. There was nothing ahead but open water, and the coast of Michigan eighty miles away.

I checked that we had lashed Lagerfeld's and Greene's cruiser tightly enough to ours and that the tires we used for bumpers were in place between us. The CPD doesn't like its boats banged up. I heard Bennis say into the radio, "We'll hold the boat," meaning the cruiser. Bennis would stay on our boat. I was guarding the scene of the crime—or what could potentially be a crime. We had agreed to this in a glance, without a word. Bennis and I have been together long enough to communicate without speaking.

I said to the two men, "Okay, now tell me again. What happened to her?"

"Oh, God!" Collum groaned. "She was so beautiful! And she must be *dead!*"

His voice was that of a soul in genuine torment, grief-filled and raw. I reminded myself that he was a very fine actor.

"Tell me what exactly happened."

"We had finished the scene," Lagerfeld said. "It was our third time through, and I thought it was fine. With this kind of a scene, really torrid, if you do it too much, it doesn't get better."

"I see."

"So I told them it was a wrap. It was the last bit to be filmed for the picture. Collum turned to go get dressed, and he said something about celebrating, and Emeraude was stretching and reaching for her robe. Glad to get it over with, I think. She must've just put her arms in the sleeves—"

"Must have? You didn't see?"

"Well, no. I was setting the camera down."

"Did you see, Mr. Greene?"

"Yes."

"You tell me what happened next."

"Um. She leaned back against the rail while she was tying the belt of her robe. And—I don't know. A wave may have hit the side of the boat. It was calm, but maybe there was a wave from some ship. I didn't see one. It would have had to be pretty far away, but there are waves sometimes that come along and you don't see what caused them—"

Lagerfeld said, "Get to the point, Collum."

"Well, she pitched backward over the rail. Just like that! It was so fast I just stared for a second or two. I mean it was like in *The Deep* where the wife just vanishes from the lifeboat while the husband is looking ahead—or maybe it's *Beast*—?"

"Go on with it," Lagerfeld said.

"So I ran to the side and looked over and I couldn't see her. I grabbed the life preserver, the round one, off the wall bracket and threw it in. Then I grabbed one of the vest types and jumped in. I swam around looking for her for—for just about forever—and then finally we decided we'd better go for help."

I said, "And you never saw her surface?"

"I never saw her after she went over the rail. I heard a

89

couple of splashes before I got to the rail and that was all. She must have sunk like a stone."

"She had put on a long terry-cloth bathrobe," Lagerfeld told me. "Maybe it dragged her down."

"And you, Mr. Lagerfeld—you didn't dive in?"

"I can't swim."

A helicopter whump-whumped over us. Collum, Lagerfeld, and I sat at the table in the cabin of their boat.

"There was a story on Channel Four news at noon that she was going to pull out of your next picture. Did you three have an argument?"

"No! We never heard it!" Collum said.

"We didn't watch the news," Lagerfeld stated more firmly and less agitatedly. "Over lunch we critiqued the last shot."

I noticed with mounting suspicion that he did not say "Omigod! You mean she planned to pull out of *Dark Passage*?"

Lagerfeld pointed at the small television set on the table. "That monitor's probably why you thought we watched the news. We use it to play our tapes through for checking."

"Does it pick up the local TV?"

I was convinced Collum started to say no, but he had hardly drawn a breath when Lagerfeld said, "It can. But we didn't watch. We were working! I told you, we spent the whole lunch critiquing the morning's filming."

"Anyhow," Collum continued, "after lunch we did the scene over again. Emeraude wouldn't have done that if we'd had a fight, would she?"

"I guess not. Can you show me the film?"

"Well, it's uh—"

"A nude love scene," Lagerfeld said.

I was about to tell them I knew about sex and stuff like

that, but you're not supposed to get sarcastic with the public. Fortunately, Lagerfeld jumped at the chance, and I had the feeling that I was being manipulated. Did they actually *want* me to see the tape, to prove they'd made it?

They turned on the monitor. Yes, the scene was steamy. Emeraude was a glossy, tawny woman, with tan skin and very blond hair. Collum was pale-skinned with red hair. They were quite a sexy pair of lovers. Collum was naked, but no frontal views. Emeraude wore nothing and was seen from all angles. This apparently reflects current values in some way.

"It isn't film you know," Lagerfeld said apologetically. "It's tape."

"What's the difference?"

"Film gives better definition. But Emeraude wouldn't do the scene in front of anybody else. At all. No crew."

"So that's why just the two of you."

"Yes. Plus, we had to get way out in the lake, out of sight of buildings and other boats. I had to do the cinematography alone, so basically we were limited to tape. Film is so much more cumbersome to get right. The lighting is much more tricky. I wouldn't have been able to do it by myself. I hope the tape's going to look compatible with the film in the final—" He stopped, realizing that he was worrying about the movie, when he should be worrying about Emeraude.

We saw all three scenes. We were inside the little cabin, and even so there was a hood over the screen to keep the bright spill of daylight off the image. Lagerfeld had filmed— taped—from many angles, apparently dashing from port to starboard while his two stars made love on the deck in the sun. In the second take the angles were different and included a lot of shots he must have made sitting on the roof over the cabin. Then the third and last time through he filmed from the deck.

While we watched, the helicopter passed over again, and I could hear Bennis on our boat sending his suggestions through the mobile relay.

The third love scene came to an end. "That's it," Lagerfeld said.

"How long does one scene take to film?"

"Oh, half an hour or so, but we talk it through first. An hour altogether."

"So you taped the first scene when?"

"About ten."

"And the second?"

"About eleven."

"And the third?"

"We broke for an hour's lunch."

"Where did you eat?"

"Out on the deck. Emeraude and Collum wanted to go right ahead while they were still made up and in costume, so to speak."

"And you filmed the third at what time?"

"About one."

"So you were finished about two?"

"Right."

And they'd approached our boat, screaming, at 2:13, or 1413 hours as the CPD and the military say. You couldn't fault the two men's testimony on the time element.

Collum said suddenly, "Why are we just sitting here? Why aren't we looking for her?" He went out on deck and Lagerfeld and I followed.

I said, "The helicopter can cover a lot more area a lot faster."

Bennis had been standing on the deck of the CPD boat listening to us in between transmissions. The deck of the cruiser was a little lower, and he leaned down to us over the rail. "A second helicopter just took off from Glenview Naval Air Station, Mr. Greene."

"Oh. Good."

Bennis glanced at me, knowing my suspicions. "Mr. Greene, we're out here right where you think it happened. You said there's a life preserver floating around someplace?"

"A—a ring life preserver and one of those orange vest things. Both. I threw one to her and then took one in when I jumped in."

"I don't see them. The helicopter doesn't see them either."

"Maybe it was farther out," Lagerfeld said.

"Like how far out?"

"I don't know. It's all just water out there."

I heard Bennis saying, "Forty-five seventy-two."

"Go ahead seventy-two."

"Try farther east. My informant isn't sure how far."

I turned to Lagerfeld. "Couldn't you have called for help on the ship-to-shore?"

"We don't have one."

"All this filming equipment and you don't have a radio?"

"It's a rented boat," he said sharply, and then wiped the annoyance from his voice. "We didn't know we'd need one."

"Of course! How could we know there was going to be an accident?"

Lagerfeld shot Collum a glance and he shut up. None of us spoke. Collum shrugged and the two men went back into the cabin to sit down.

Collum Greene was nervous. In fact, Lagerfeld was nervous, too, though he showed it less, but to what extent did nervousness indicate guilt? A lot of perfectly innocent people can't even say hello to a police officer without stuttering and fidgeting, let alone somebody who has just been involved in a suspicious death. My instinct, however, was that they were guilty of more than watching Emeraude pitch backward overboard. How could I jog them a little?

Bennis was on the radio again with the Coast Guard, and we could see the helicopter making a slow run east from our position.

Bennis said into his radio, "It may have been even farther east than that—well, give it a try."

The rules are you can question witnesses without cautioning them. If you question suspects, you have to give them the Miranda warning. If I gave these two famous people the Miranda warning, it could make them very angry, and they would have no trouble kicking up a fit in the media. Stars understand media. CHICAGO COPS BULLY ACTOR AND DIRECTOR. Wonderful! I didn't have much time to make a decision about what to do. Whichever I did could be wrong and could botch up the case.

And then my name would be mud.

However, right now they were rattled. They may have made up this story, and if so, it was still new to them and they wouldn't know whether it would fly. By the time they got to shore, they would have perfected it by rehearsing it on me.

I wandered over to the rail of the cruiser. Bennis leaned down closer to me over the rail of the CPD boat. I asked softly, "What do you think?"

"I think they pitched her in the drink."

"It's just their word. I mean, there's no evidence."

Bennis said, "Even if her body's found, there won't be. Not if she just drowned. If we don't find a bullet in her head. Which I doubt. These guys are not idiots. Impulsive maybe, but not idiots. Who's to say from a drowned body whether these characters were throwing life preservers at her while she drowned or driving the boat in the opposite direction?"

"Hell!"

"Well, I hate to have them get away, too, but what are you going to do?"

"What about the tapes? Say they made the first tape at ten, the second at eleven, the third at twelve. Then say they heard the news, got pissed off, and pushed her overboard. Then say they waited until about two, just to be on the safe side, and then went roaring off screaming for help. If we could prove the three filmings were done before lunch, we'd have them cold."

"I don't see how you'd do that."

"The angle of the light? At eleven the sun is a little to the east and at one it's moved farther west."

"Yes, but the boat can motor around and face any which way. You won't be able to tell that unless you get some city background in the shot to tell you. Was there?"

I shook my head. "No. Just deck and a little water beyond the railing."

"If we had a consistent chop from one direction, you might get an idea which way the boat was facing. But as far as I can remember, it's been glassy calm all day."

"Glassy calm in the tape, too. Damn!" Bennis had a radio call and turned away.

I didn't believe their story. It was all just too convenient. The breaking news, Emeraude's threat. I looked up at the bright yellow furnace of the sun for inspiration.

And found it.

I went back into the cruiser cabin.

Lagerfeld and Collum were still nervous. They had not been talking together while I had talked with Bennis. They were beyond earshot in the cabin, but I had watched them out of the corner of my eye. Probably they didn't want to look like they were colluding. I sauntered casually—as casually as possible on a boat deck—over to them. Then I just stood next to them, gazing out at the lake. The second helicopter was now quartering the area in tandem with the first. A Coast Guard cutter appeared from the south.

My presence made the two men more nervous.

"You say you took a break for lunch?"

Collum jumped and Lagerfeld blinked. "Yes, I had a sandwich," Collum said.

Lagerfeld said, "I think Emeraude didn't even eat. She was a little seasick."

I glanced pointedly at the extremely calm water.

"Or maybe dieting," he added.

Or maybe they were trying to cover for the fact that Emeraude's body would be found with no food in the stomach. Maybe she had drowned before they got around to lunch. The news item had been on at 12:07, 1207 hours.

I said, "So did you stay in your—ah—acting garb for lunch?" Birthday suit.

Collum tossed his handsome head. "Sure. It didn't seem worth it to dress. And like I said before, we were rehearsing."

"And the final tape was shot at one?"

"One, one-fifteen. Something like that."

I pounced.

"So, when we get your tapes enlarged, they'll show you a lot more sunburned in the third version than you were in the first two run-throughs?"

Collum's mouth dropped open. Lagerfeld's eyes narrowed.

Collum said, "I guess—"

"I wonder. It's odd that your arm is turning red up to the sleeve. White underneath."

I pointed, not touching him, at the sunburn that went up

his arm and ended at the short sleeve of his shirt. "You'd think an easy-burning redhead like you had had that shirt on a couple of hours now. Since, oh, maybe noon?"

Collum stared.

But Lagerfeld, who was smarter than Collum, spoke up. "He did it! He pushed her in and ran into the cabin and grabbed the wheel and drove away from her. And by the time I got hold of the wheel and came back, I couldn't find her."

"That's a lie!" Collum shouted.

"And then I was scared that the police would blame us both, so I went along with his story. I mean, he was the one who wet his hair and said he'd been diving for her. I didn't tell on him, but I never hurt her."

"No, he did it!" Collum said. "He was screaming at her because she was pulling out of *Dark Passage* and he'd lose his backing and all the money he's put in it so far."

The helicopter sighted the life preserver and life vest quite a bit more to the east. A couple of days later, Emeraude's body was sighted, considerably farther north. Either she'd drifted, or they'd motored a mile or two before dumping the life preservers in the lake.

Bennis and I wrapped the case up. With both Collum Greene and Steven Lagerfeld accusing each other, it was never possible to decide who did which thing first. My guess was that Lagerfeld and Emeraude argued, struggled, and she fell overboard, whereupon he and Collum both just decided not to go in after her. It turned out that Collum had backed the *Dark Passage* project heavily with his own money and was every bit as angry at her as Lagerfeld. I could bring myself to believe that after she went down, they relented and tried to find her, then panicked, then made up a good story. They were charged with manslaughter, which seemed about right to me.

Our commander was amazed and delighted, which is one
of the best things that police commanders can be. Then they
make flattering notes that get filed in your personnel jacket.

The regular Marine Unit personnel recovered from their
attack of salmonella in two days, which was a pity. As I said,
to Bennis, "I could cruise around out here another week, best
buddy."

"Suze, my man. Likewise."

My husband, Tony, thought up this title. Then he said, "Well, I've done the hard work. Now all you have to do is pencil in the story that goes with it."

If You've Got the Money, Honey, I've Got the Crime

Eight or ten of the third watch were standing around in a clump outside the roll call room door. It wasn't considered the thing to do, to file in early and sit meekly in the seats. Instead, the officers hung around outside talking, and they'd go piling in through the door at the very last minute. This always annoyed Sergeant Pat Touhy, which was exactly what it was supposed to do. Touhy folded her arms and glanced with exaggerated patience out the high windows at the amber sodium vapor street lighting that ran along State Street, making the pavement look Venusian and the dark beyond look purple. A few flakes of snow fell, briefly visible as they passed through the light, then vanishing into the dark.

In the hall, Officer Hiram Quail had spent some time talking about a river in Michigan, the Pere Marquette, where he loved to go when he had a few days off, or even just a weekend, and fish for rainbow trout. It made a change, Quail said, from Chicago. And Officer Stanley Mileski said, "You can embroider that on a sampler!" Then Norm Bennis described the last event of his and Susannah Maria Figueroa's tour last night. Figueroa was a short, energetic white woman of twenty-five. Bennis was a stocky black man, ten years older, who had twelve years on the job, compared to Figueroa's three. He considered himself her mentor. So did she, some of the time.

99

"The grocer, this little Korean guy," Bennis said, lounging with his left shoulder against the cinderblock wall, "he has a deal with his wife upstairs, she's sittin' up with the baby. They got no store alarm, nothin' like that. Too expensive, or maybe he don't think we'll come, who knows? So if he's gettin' held up, he pushes this button, buzzer sounds upstairs, not in the store, wife calls the cops on her phone."

"Which is not a bad idea," Figueroa said.

"So last night he sees this seriously evil-looking pair come in his store. Chains, black leather with Satan on the back, tattoos, like they're putting a sign up, 'Please arrest me.' They're slouching around lookin' at stuff, see. Grocer pushes his private panic button. Our bad men don't hear it, see, but upstairs the wife calls the police. So Figueroa and me we get the call and we go screamin' over there, like there's an armed robbery in progress, and we go bustin' into the place, the two evildoers are standing there smiling."

"I *hate* that in a crook," Mileski said.

"Absolutely nothin' has happened. One's looking at the videos, is he gonna rent *Grease* or is he gonna rent a skin flick. The other one is deciding between Cheerios and maybe a healthy hot cereal like Wheatena. The shopkeeper has to admit they ain't pulled a firearm yet, and we pat 'em down, they don't have gun one. Meanwhile, one of 'em's saying, 'Well, I know you have to do your duty, officer, but I think maybe my civil rights are being violated here.' This is education at Joliet for you. The other one says do we have probable cause."

"Probable cause!" Figueroa said. "I ask you."

"So by then even the shopkeeper has to admit everything's copacetic, and we stand around with the two non-perps and the Korean, shoot the shit a little, the non-perps do some shoppin', buy a package of cigarettes is all, we look around the store a little and the Korean offers me a Milky Way, but hell, I'm on a diet—"

"Coulda given it to me," Figueroa said.

"And we're about to leave, Figueroa says, 'Hey!' to me. She's pointin' at the non-perps and I gotta admit I don't see anything wrong.

"She says, 'I woulda guessed that guy 5'10" a hundred and forty pounds we came in. Looks one-seventy now.' Damn if she isn't right. Other one's gained a little weight, too.

" 'Hey, boys,' I say, 'gimme just another feel for those guns.'

"Well, they start to run. We flip 'em both, prone 'em out on the floor, and whaddya know. They got shirt pockets, pants pockets, jacket pockets, jockstraps, everything just fulla stuff. They got chocolate bars in the shirt, already gettin' warm, cans of pickled octopus, package of steak strips in the jacket, one of 'em's got videos all around inside his belt. Other one, he's like got a hard-on, I think, but turns out it's a cucumber. And what really gets to me is this: They picked all this crap up while we were talkin' with the Korean and all of us were wanderin' around the store. Is this *bad?* I mean, what kind of idiots do they think we are, we're gonna let them walk out with a couple hundred dollars' worth of groceries in their pants?"

"Sounds like they almost got away with it," Stanley Mileski said.

"Well, yeah. If Figueroa didn't have such a *fashion-conscious* mind, yeah. I guess they woulda."

"You search 'em, Figueroa?" Mileski asked.

Hiram Quail said, "Pat 'em down, did you?"

Mileski said, "Give 'em the giggles; feel 'em up?"

Quail said, "Course, they'd hardly know the difference,

male or female, in that uniform."

"Unisex, that's the Chicago Police Department," Mileski said.

"Basically, you look like a really short guy."

"Oh, drop it, Mileski." Figueroa brushed them both off and went into the roll call room. But at the same time, she knew it was true. Except for the difficulty of stuffing female hips and busts into the dark blue pants and shirt, there was nothing particularly edifying about the uniform. And the Chicago Police Department gave women two choices for hairstyles: A. Short. B. Tied up under the cap. Figueroa currently was wearing a very short ponytail.

Norm sidled over and sat next to her. He said, "Don't worry about those guys." She appreciated it, but she was still annoyed.

She was well aware that this was a sensitive area to her. And she couldn't let them see they could push her buttons on it or they'd never stop. Figueroa had grown up in a half-Mexican, half-Italian family—as one friend said, "Just destined to be calm and placid, weren't you?" Traditional roles were important for her older relatives. Nobody but her sister had been supportive at all when Suze decided to be a cop. In fact, they had been horrified. It was unfeminine. Her mother said, "Susannah, you won't look pretty." Both her Mexican and her Italian relatives thought white confirmation dresses with ruffles from top to bottom were the standard against which all female clothing should be judged.

Suze herself, while presenting a tough, decisive front to her uncles, aunts, grandparents, mother and father, nourished a small worm of doubt. Maybe her choices in life *were* unfeminine.

Maybe she was wrong. A divorce the year after she joined the department hadn't helped any, either. Still, she thought she was nice-looking, if not gorgeous, and by God, she was going to do a job that interested her, not just sit around like a cupcake.

Roll call ran its usual course. Sergeant Pat Touhy, herself a tall, strong-looking woman, read some crimes. Also one section of the Illinois constitution, which was today's lesson for the troops. Touhy had printed it on the blackboard, which stood next to the car assignment sheets and asked several officers to explain phrases out of it. The Chicago Police Department took cop education medium seriously.

Suze sat through the whole thing with her arms folded, her forehead frowning and her mind grumpy. She wasn't called on, and it was a good thing.

When Touhy gave them the word to hit the bricks and clear, Figueroa and Bennis took off into the night in their old reliable squad car, designated 1-33, meaning first district, car thirty-three.

Figueroa drove. Pretty soon, the seriously macho mars lights and the seriously macho radio and the seriously macho dash equipment started to make her feel better. Their beat ran along Michigan Avenue past the Chicago Hilton and Towers, the Art Institute and some of the priciest lake frontage in the world. Then they swung back under the El, looking for homeless sleeping and maybe freezing in small, dark, hidden places behind Dumpsters. Snow continued to sift past the streetlights, but melted on the ground.

Not fifteen minutes out of the lot, at 1131 hours, Bennis and Figueroa saw three men talking huddled in a doorway off south State. One of the men was distinctly better dressed than the other two. Figueroa stopped the car half a block farther along—the dome light was turned off, of course, so that it wouldn't go on when they got out of the car—and she and Bennis walked up on the men and surprised them, Bennis going around the block and coming in from behind.

Five minutes later they were calling the dispatcher.

Bennis said, "1-33."

"Thirty-three, go."

"I've got three in custody from a drug arrest and no cage. We need another car to transport the third offender."

Mileski, who was alone in his car tonight, took the third perp. Figueroa and Bennis spent half an hour in the station on the paper and then they were out again.

"Not exactly your difficult bust," Figueroa said.

"Sitting ducks."

"Like taking candy from a baby."

"*However,* quite pleasant for the old personnel file."

The dispatcher said, "1-33."

Suze said, "Thirty-three."

"I have a number-two parker at—"

Norm, who was driving now, swung the wheel. "Watch, it'll be a car in a handicapped zone."

"Ten cents says bus stop."

Meanwhile, the dispatcher said, "1-27."

Mileski said, "Twenty-seven."

"I have a car blocking the alley at 126 North Rush."

"Ten ninety-nine."

By the time Bennis and Figueroa had dealt with their car, Bennis winning the dime because it was indeed a handicapped zone, they heard Mileski call for a tow.

Then the dispatcher said, "1-33."

Suze answered, "Thirty-three."

"We have a disturbance at the Kountry Klub Lounge, 621 north Franklin. That's 621 north on Franklin."

"Ten-four, squad."

"Let us know if you need backup. Seems to be a fight. Bartender called it in."

★ ★ ★ ★ ★

Norm had always told Suze that the main thing cops did was walk into a situation *in control*. When the civilians were too zonked or too crooked or too angry or too nuts or too injured to cope, cops coped.

Suze walked into the Kountry Klub Lounge in a mood to cope.

After the cold outdoors, Suze felt she had sunk into a pillow of warm beer fumes. The Kountry Klub may have intended to be country, but it had its metaphors a little mixed and had more western than Nashville in its decor. Inside the front door was a saguaro cactus made of green denim with ties of black thread representing needles. It was taller than Norm. There were skulls from longhorn cattle over the bar to Suze's right, an occasional Navajo blanket on the walls, and the dividers at the two edges of the stage, which was at the farthest end of the room, were split-rail fencing. The stage was brightly lit. A drummer was sitting, bored but patient, behind his drums on a raised dais, also bordered with split-rail fencing. Three exotically dressed women sat together on the edge of the dais near the drummer. The apron stage was a large expanse of blond wood twenty feet wide and fifteen deep, raised maybe three feet above the dance-floor/audience-floor level.

Lying in the center of the stage, sparkling in the spotlights, was a glass hypodermic syringe.

Closer to Norm and Suze, in the somewhat darker area intended for the audience, people were milling around and shouting. Looking at them, Figueroa thought, Whoa! There's never been so much denim in such a small space outside of the Levi's factory shipping room. There was denim studded with metal stars and denim coated with rhinestones. Embroidered denim. Slashed denim. Red denim. Even denim shot through with Mylar threads. Suze took stock. Several members of the audience were damaged, one with a bloody nose, another with a deep cut over a cheekbone that was oozing blood, a third with a scalp cut that was *pouring* blood. On the floor, four men were sitting on another guy who was rolling around—trying to roll around, Suze mentally corrected herself—and screaming assorted obscenities. The bartender wore a striped shirt with sleeve garters and a white apron. He went right on serving drinks.

Without consulting each other, Norm and Suze worked as a team, Norm stopping in the doorway and putting out a call on his radio for the paramedics, Suze walking forward and saying, "Now, who can tell me what happened here?"

A woman said, "This man, he was playing and singing, and then—"

"Just jumped down and started swinging at everybody," the man with the bloody cheek said.

"Hey, you yelled at him first, guy," said the man with the cut scalp.

Suze nodded and studied the singer, who was writhing on the floor. He wore Levi's, ones so tight that, even though he was thrashing back and forth and shrieking, he couldn't bring his knees up to his chest. He wore a western-fringed leather vest, cut shorter than usual, with dangles of turquoise and silver on the ends of the fringe. Under it nothing. No shirt, just heavy-duty pecs and lats, deltoids, and biceps on the arms, and a sheen that was either oil or perspiration. Suze classified him: hunk type, makes good use of it.

Bennis came up behind her. "You find the manager," he said. "I'll look after little buddy here."

The only person in the place who was dressed like normal folks turned out to be the stage manager, and he was standing next to a light board a couple steps below stage level, off stage left. He responded immediately to Suze's questions. This was a man, she thought, who liked things to proceed on schedule and was unhappy with the present unpleasantness.

"What's the deal here?" she said.

"Your basic fight, I guess," he said.

"Who's been fighting?"

"Mainly Hank. Hank's the act."

"Yeah, I saw the sign on the way in. 'Hank Benton with Faith, Hope and Charity.' "

"That's him. He's a regular with us. He's popular here."

"Not with everybody. The guy over there said somebody in the audience insulted him."

The manager said, "Yeah, well, he was acting funny before that, is why."

"Starting from when?"

"Well, see, he sings eight songs then takes a break. Then he sings another eight. You know. So this one is the finale of this set, 'If You've Got the Money, Honey, I've Got the Time.' His fave, I guess. See, he liked to open this number by me cutting the lights out everyplace." The manager added hastily, "I don't mean the exit lights. We always have them on. But the houselights and stage lights I cut. So he does the first four chords in the dark. Dramatic, he thinks. Then the lights come up and he goes real quick into the song. Which went okay. It wasn't until, uh, maybe close to the end he started making these whooping noises. They weren't in the number, way he usually did it. Then he started doing funny little steps, like making fun o' the song. Which this crowd doesn't like. I mean, we aren't into satire here, you know?"

"Okay," said Figueroa.

"And so somebody said something. Like 'Cut out the stupid shit' or like that. And he yelled back at them. And they yelled back at him. And he dumped the guitar there and jumped into the crowd and started swinging at everybody."

"I see. Why did he do that?"

"Well, jeez," the manager said. He pointed at the syringe. "He took something that didn't agree with him. Right?"

"I guess," she said cautiously. "Has it been moved?"

"It was lying there when the lights came up for the song. Nobody's touched it."

Figueroa was beginning to wonder whether Hank had really injected himself, no matter how it looked. Somehow she could not picture Hank himself bringing that syringe on-stage. At the same time, she wasn't quite sure why the picture was so wrong. Figueroa detested the notion of feminine intuition, but she was willing to believe that "cop sense" told her there was an unresolved problem here.

She studied the audience. About half were crowded around Hank and the paramedics, enjoying the unscheduled show. The other half were taking the opportunity to imbibe a little extra alcohol and blunt the rigors of winter in Chicago. Nobody seemed grieved by Hank's collapse.

The manager said, "Can you get him outa here? We got a club to run."

"But nobody to sing."

"The backups can handle half an hour. I got another singer I can call." He smiled sourly. "No lack of out-of-work singers."

Suze pointed at the three women near the drummer. "Those his backup singers?" Well, obviously they were. What else could they be?

"Yeah. Faith, Hope and Charity."

"Uh, is there any unpleasantness, like among the performers?"

"In show business? Unpleasantness? Jealousy? Backbiting? You must be kidding!"

"Like what?"

"Well, Faith just got dumped by Hank the Great. As a girl-friend, I mean. Hope is gonna be fired by Hank because he doesn't think she can sing. This is her last night. Charity wants to go off on her own. And she could, she's good enough, except she's under contract to Hank while the act is here."

"Doesn't Hope have a contract, too?"

"Yeah, but Hank says, 'Sue me,' and she doesn't have the money to sue, plus it'll look bad for her, career-wise. Getting fired. Country singing—even *fake* country singing," he said with a sneer, "is a small world. Hank has the money and the power. The more fuss she makes, the more people hear about it. The drummer hates Hank's guts, too, by the way."

"Why?"

"Stole his girlfriend. Then threw her over for Faith. Who he then dumped, too."

"Sweet fellow, Hank."

"The finest."

"What happens when a performer shoots up onstage and screws up a performance?"

"We just might dump *him*."

"Thanks."

Figueroa walked across the stage to the three women. She glanced briefly at the syringe as she passed it, but left it lying where it was. One mustached kid from the audience was eyeing it. As Suze walked past, she said to him in a stage whisper, "Don't even *think* about touching it." He flinched back. The syringe was four inches long, five counting the needle. Several feet away from it, at the stage apron, lay a silver electric guitar, one of the latest kind, practically all strings and pickups.

As Figueroa approached the women, she could see that the visual motif of this act, costume-wise, was fringe.

"Who is who?" she asked.

"I'm Deloris Michael," one said.

"And in the act?"

"Faith."

Faith was dressed in a bodysuit of see-through white lace. It was made of lace-printed stretch fabric, and covered her from neck to ankle like paint. A fringe about two inches long ran around her at hipbone level. Figueroa doubted whether Faith had any underwear on under the bodysuit and didn't want to stare, but she was suddenly quite sure that Hank had chosen it for exactly that reason. The male audience would spend the whole act trying to tell. She wore high-heeled silvery shoes. Her face was heavily made up in pastel colors—pale pink lipstick, pale blue eyelids, pale skin. Against this, her hair was black, cut moderately short and loosely curled.

"My, my!" Bennis said, approaching Suze, but looking at Faith. Suze stepped back half a pace, offended. To cover her annoyance, she glanced around and saw the paramedics had arrived. They had loosened Hank's Levi's at the waist, which seemed to her to be an excellent idea.

Hope—Lorelei Smith—was gilded. She was sleek, slender, small-breasted and gold all over. Fringed gold bikini top and bottom. Gold high heels. Short glossy gold hair. Gold skin.

"Is that paint?" Figueroa said, pointing at the gold color on Hope's leg.

"Naw. Hank wanted me to get painted, but somebody told me if you paint yourself gold your skin can't breathe and you die. Actually, I oil myself—" She ran a fingertip slowly up from her knee to her hip to demonstrate. Figueroa heard Bennis say "Uhnnn" behind her. "Just a little oil, and then I kinda sift this gold glitter on and it sticks."

Bennis said to Suze, "Look at her. Puts you in mind of Hogarth's Gin Lane and the bizarre excesses at the court of Louis XIII, don't it, Figueroa?"

"Bennis, you're weird."

"I'm weird but I'm cute."

She gave him a look intended to chasten, which made him chuckle.

Charity—Sue Gleason—was yet another type, and Figueroa began to see a kind of sly intelligence operating in the choice of names and costumes. Faith was all in white lace, but Figueroa suspected that nobody would say she looked particularly faithful. Hope was golden. Charity—well, jeez! Figueroa thought—looked like a caricature of what every man would wish somebody would give him as a gift. BIG breasts. Small waist. Lush hips. A corset-style red costume, like something out of an old wild West movie. Two-inch fringe around the top and bottom of the corset, also red. Red lips, red nails, red high heels. Her hair was red too, combed straight with no hint of curl, very lustrous, hanging just below her chin.

Between the three of them, Figueroa thought this was like her own personal nightmare come to life. Here were women who could hardly walk because of the high heels, whose own faces were invisible under the makeup, who you wouldn't know if you met them on the street the next day, but every male in the place was fascinated. Put them outdoors chasing a mugger and they'd be flat on their faces in two steps. Grimly, Figueroa asked Faith, "How long does it take you to put on all that makeup? Not the lace suit, but the eyelashes and the hair and all?"

"Oh, forty-five minutes."

"Forty-five minutes!"

"Yeah. I know it's kinda surprising I can do it that fast. But I've had a lot of experience."

"So what kind of a guy is this Hank?"

"A real turd," said Hope, the gilded one.

"Why?"

"He lies a lot. Promises you things and doesn't follow through."

Faith said, "Yeah. That's his style. Baits you, you know, with how he's gonna help you."

Hope said, "I mean, people warned me. But he seems so sincere when he talks with you. You believe him."

"He sings sincere too," Faith said. "They're both an act."

Figueroa said to Charity, who hadn't spoken, "What about you?"

Charity said, "Hank Benton is slime on a stick."

Figueroa nodded, slightly startled. "What do you three do in the act? Can you tell me?"

"Better," Faith said. They stepped apart, singing "money, honey, money, honey" half a dozen times, swung their upper bodies around, swooped their heads in circles, hair flashing in the lights, fringes swinging, then sang "Ooooooh-ooh-ooh-ooh!" as they came back together. They put their arms around each other's waists and ended with a "Hmmmmmmmmmmm."

Figueroa said, "Well, thanks. Hang on. I'll be right back."

She walked into the audience area with Bennis at her heels. "Let's wrap this up," he said. "Management's getting antsy."

"Not yet. We don't know what happened."

"Ol' Hank just screwed up is all."

"I don't believe it. Give me a minute."

Hank had stopped thrashing around—whether in the natural course of things by tiring himself out, or because of something the medics had done, Suze didn't know. He was sitting up, but still cursing. The paramedics were checking out the man with the cut scalp and the man with the cut cheek. Figueroa studied Hank. There were no needle tracks so far as she could see on his arms. He had a good deal here at the Kountry Klub. And she deduced from the care he took with his backup singers' costumes that he was very serious about his act. Would he have risked it all to shoot up onstage? But who else could have carried the syringe through a whole set of songs?

There was a reddish rash across the middle of Hank's mostly bare torso. It ran along the area where the turquoise and silver things dangled at the ends of his fringe. She felt the silver pieces. They were bent and faceted to pick up stage lights, but they had sharp corners. Obviously, they poked his skin. Anyone of the rash-bumps could be the place something was injected—by Hank or by an enemy of Hank's? There was a largish one on his chest, just under his left elbow, that looked different from the others—bigger, but less red. If he was right-handed, he could have injected himself there. Figueroa pointed to it and Bennis nodded.

"Is he right-handed?" she asked one of the bystanders.

"He plays right-handed."

"So he could have done it himself," Bennis said quietly to her.

"Or someone onstage, in the dark before the last song."

If so, who? Figueroa thought she knew.

"He must've did it himself," Hope said. She patted at some flaws in the gold glitter on her arms.

Figueroa studied Bennis out of the corner of her eye. It was what he believed also, but to Hope she said, "Oh, no he didn't. He couldn't have brought the syringe onstage. He didn't have enough room in that costume to hide two nickels.

He wasn't wearing a hat to keep it in. And he couldn't have brought it in his guitar because it's not acoustic. It's electric and it's as flat as a paper plate."

"Underneath?" said Faith, the one in lace.

"Underneath the guitar? Nope. He would've had to hold it against his stomach all evening. That's not the way you people play." She saw Bennis raise his eyebrows in agreement. For him, that was a lot of reaction.

"Any of us could have done it," Charity said. "Bring it in under our hair, maybe."

"Nope. Faith's is too short, Hope's is *much* too short and yours is cut wrong. It's straight. You shake your heads in your act. It just wouldn't work. Now, if you had *big* hair, like Dolly Parton—"

Charity said, "Maybe the drummer did it?"

"Oh, please. Get out from behind all that stuff in the dark and come down off the dais in the dark and find Hank in the dark and inject him and get back up there in the dark, while he plays just four chords? Four seconds, tops! What kind of idiots do you think we—"

Bennis said, "Figueroa," in a cautionary tone. You didn't want any bizarre behavior to get back to the commander.

"Same for your stage manager. Not enough time to get out there, find Hank, inject him, get back and hit the lights. Had to be somebody next to him on the stage."

Faith, Hope and Charity looked at each other.

Figueroa said, "Kind of smart, really, to inject him in the side. He didn't notice, more than to be annoyed, because he was used to those stupid—uh, those silver and turquoise dangles sticking him all the time." And that made it worse, Figueroa thought, that the attacker was smart. That she was smart and didn't have anything better to do with her brains than this.

Faith said, "Well, but you can't tell who."

"Yes, I can. Only one person could have brought the syringe onstage. Nobody else had room."

Charity said, "*Nobody* had room. Lookit these costumes." Her red corset was as tight as the skin on a hot dog.

"Faith is covered by a body stocking, a smooth, transparent body stocking. And Hope's covered mainly by glitter. But you had room. In your cleavage. And I'm ashamed—" Figueroa strangled the impulse to say "I'm ashamed of you." Charity hadn't noticed. She was hopping from foot to foot and yelling. Bennis' eyebrows went up and down with the bouncing breasts.

"Oh, no I didn't!" Charity yelled. "And you can't prove I did."

Figueroa had a moment's qualm. Hank was surely a nasty bit of humankind. Was Figueroa betraying sisterhood? God only knew. God only knew and She was far too pissed these days to tell anybody.

Bennis was a hundred percent with her now. He said to Charity, "C'mere a second." They walked Charity aside.

Bennis and Figueroa went into their one-two punch mode. Figueroa said, "Listen, Charity. Um, Sue. Syringes can be traced."

Bennis said, "She's right. Also drugs—prescription or illegals. Either one."

"Plus fingerprints on the syringe."

"It's gonna go better for you if you tell the paramedics what you used. Help them out."

"I didn't do it."

"See," Bennis said, as if she hadn't spoken, "you are talking here to a coupla street cops with a lotta years in. I mean, drug diagnosis is our thing."

Figueroa said, "Yeah," though she knew Bennis had the

years of knowledge, not her.

"I mean," Bennis said, "suppose, just suppose, you gave him some kinda speed, say meth maybe."

Charity's eyes flickered to Hank and back, but she didn't say anything.

Bennis said, "Now, suppose you were judging the dose by what experienced users can take. A thousand, maybe two thousand milligrams at once. And suppose he wasn't a chronic user—which would be the reason you used it, 'cause you knew he would overreact. Well, did you know that 120 milligrams is fatal in non-users?"

Charity's mouth opened a little wider.

Figueroa said, "Yeah. If you overdosed him and he dies and you coulda saved him, you'll be in extremely deep shit."

Bennis said, "And plus, if he dies it's murder. Right now, worst, you got some kinda assault. If he lives."

Figueroa said, "And here you were, trying to shoot him up in the dark. You're trying to skin-pop him, but you couldn't see. Maybe it went in a vein, which might be why it took hold so fast. Maybe it went right to his heart. We're talking possible murder here, no matter how careful you thought you were being." She paused and added, "Your contract calls for you to back up Hank as long as he runs here. You had a chance at a real career—you're the one with talent—and he had you locked in. Unless the Kountry Klub fired him."

"I don't suppose," Bennis said, "you were all three in it together?"

Charity sighed, draping her extremely long eyelashes down over her cheeks. They reached almost to her cheekbones. Suze and Norm said nothing whatever now, just staring at her.

"Oh, shit," Charity said. "No, don't blame them. And yeah, it's meth. Kinda hefty dose." Bennis immediately walked away to talk with the paramedics.

Liking her better, Suze said, "And Hank doesn't skin-pop?"

"No. He doesn't do drugs; he's a juicer; he does booze." A satisfied smile came over Charity's face. "Took him right up, didn't it?"

"It did that."

Twenty minutes later they'd put the incident to bed. Hank Benton was in the Northwestern Emergency Room giving the staff hell. Charity was in the First District station engaging in felony review with the state's attorney. Norm and Suze were gearing up to go back out and look for some more malefactors. Suze Figueroa was feeling a distinct sense of accomplishment. She said, "Let's go, big guy."

"You were mad at me there, weren't you?" Norm said. "When I was kind of ogling Faith."

"For a while."

"I didn't mean it."

"Which part didn't you mean?"

"All of it, matter of fact. I come in here at night, get suited up, see you waiting to hit the mean streets with me, basically." He put his arm around her shoulders. "Soon as I see you, it makes me feel good."

"Without the two-inch nails? Without the three-inch heels? Without the eyelashes?"

"Yeah. Without."

Suze said, "Okay."

Chicago is more than a city to me, it's a living, breathing, moody, exciting character. So naturally I employ that character whenever I can. Here is one of its manifestations.

Stop, Thief!

Officer Susannah Maria Figueroa lounged back against one of the desks in the roll-call room. She was five feet one, which made her just the right height to be able to rest both buttocks on the desktop.

"See—this woman in a Porsche was driving along, minding her own business, on the way to an afternoon of serious shopping," she said to Officers Hiram Quail and Stanley Mileski, while her partner, Norm Bennis, taller than she was, lounged with one thigh against a neighboring desk, "and *whump!* she hits a cat in the street."

"I would think *moosh!* Not *whump!*" Mileski said. He was a skinny white guy, slightly stooped.

"She gets out," Figueroa said, "looks at the cat, head's okay, tail's okay, but it's flat as a wafer in the middle. Well, it's about three o'clock in the afternoon and she figures the kids'll be coming outa school soon and it's gonna upset the little darlings to see a squashed cat."

"Would," said Mileski. "Some. Then again, some of 'em would love it."

"So she picks it up real careful by the tail and puts it in a Bloomingdale's bag she had in the car and drives on to the mall with it."

"Type o' woman," said Norm Bennis, "who has lotsa extra Bloomie's bags." Bennis was a black man of medium

118

height, built like a wedge. He had slender legs, broad chest, and very, very muscular shoulders.

"Right," said Figueroa, shrugging a little to settle her walkie-talkie more comfortably. "So she pulls up into the mall. Gets out to go in, she should hit Nieman Marcus before the rush starts, but the sun's shinin' down hard and she figures the car's gonna heat up and the cat's gonna get hot and smell up her car."

"Which it would," said Mileski.

"So she takes the bag and puts it up on the hood of the car to wait there while she's shopping. She goes in the mall. Meanwhile, along comes this other woman—"

"Nice lookin' lady," Bennis said. "Named Marietta."

"—who sees the bag there, thinks hah! Fine merchandise unattended, and takes it. Then this woman Marietta with the Bloomie's bag goes into the mall. She's a shoplifter. She's truckin' through the jewelry department at Houston's lookin' for something worth boostin', sees a pearl necklace some clerk didn't put back, picks it up, opens the Bloomie's bag, drops the necklace in, sees the cat, screams like a train whistle, and falls down in a dead faint. The store manager or some such honcho runs over, tries to revive her, slaps her face, but she sits up once, glances at the bag and falls over again in a dead faint, so they call the paramedics. The EMTs arrive, chuck her onto a gurney, put her Bloomie's bag between her feet, which is SOP with personal belongings, and whisk her out to the ambulance."

"Meanwhile," Bennis said, "the clerk at the jewelry counter's seen the pearls are missin'."

"Which is where we come in. By this time the woman's at the hospital, but by astute questioning of the store personnel, we put two and two together—"

"*Experience* and astute questioning, Suze my man,"

119

Bennis said. Bennis was thirty-five. Suze was twenty-six.

"—we figure out where the pearls are. So we roll on over to the hospital with lights and siren. Woman's in the emergency room and we just mosey on in and ask if we can dump out the bag. Orderly doesn't know enough to say no—"

"Sometimes you luck out," said Bennis.

"—so we turn the bag upside down and out flops the pearls plus the dead cat. At which point, the *orderly* faints."

"We were kinda surprised ourselves," Bennis said. "Didn't faint, though."

"Too tough," said Figueroa.

"Macho," said Bennis.

"Spent the next two hours in the district on the paper," Figueroa said.

"Odd, you know, when a supposed victim turns into a perp. Kinda felt sorry for her."

Figueroa said, "Not me, Bennis. She's a crook."

Mileski said, "Don't suppose they managed to revive the cat?"

Sergeant Touhy strode in and the third watch crew faded into seats.

Sergeant Touhy said, "Bennis? Figueroa? We've had a complaint from the hospital. Seems they don't like cat guts on their gurneys."

Bennis started to say, "We didn't know about the cat—" but Figueroa kicked him and muttered, "Probable cause!" so he shut up. "But we got our offender, Sarge," Suze Figueroa said.

"Yeah," Bennis said. "Boosts our solved record."

Touhy ignored them. "Next time, look in the bag first. Now let's read some crimes."

"You really need *three* ammo pouches?" Quail whispered at Figueroa. "You expecting a war?"

She whispered back. "Hey! You get in serious shit and I come in as backup you'll kiss my pouches."

Each ammo pouch held six rounds of .38 ammunition for the standard service revolver. You could fit three pouches, max, on your Sam Browne, though most officers didn't. Privately, Figueroa wished she could carry her ammo like the cowboys did, in loops all around the belt. But the department had a regulation that all ammo had to be concealed. Takes half the fun out, Figueroa thought.

She also thought it would be nice if Maintenance would wait to turn on the heat in here until the weather got cold. The roll-call room for the First District was never going to be a photo opportunity for *Architectural Digest*. But why not livable? The smell of hot wool and sweat was practically thick enough to see.

After ten minutes or so Touhy finished up with, "Pick up the new runaway list at the desk. Now, we've been getting more and more complaints from the senior-citizen groups in the neighborhood, and I'll tell you now I don't want the Gray Panthers on my ass. We got a lot of older people out there, they think they're under siege. From teenagers, more than our serious nasties. These are people who're specifically trying to get their grocery shopping done before the schools let out. Get back in their houses before the teenagers are set free. I mean, it's like three-thirty to them is when the Draculas come out. They get pushed, hassled. Yelled at. Called bad names. Get their groceries stolen."

"It happens," Mileski said.

"Not in *my* district it don't, Mileski!"

"Right, boss."

"Okay. Now hit the bricks and clear."

Norm and Suze were in an early car today, so they were on

the street by three in the afternoon. They were beat car 1-33, patrolling the north end of the district.

Chicago's First District is unique among the twenty-five district stations in that it operates out of the big central copshop at 11th and State. It is also one of the most varied districts. It has world-class hotels of mind-boggling elegance and enough marble to stress the bedrock. It has the most soul-deadening public housing. It has staggeringly expensive jewelry emporiums and meretricious underwear stores where lewd sayings are embroidered on bras and panty bottoms. It has grade schools and premier medical schools and on-the-job training in crime and prostitution.

"One thirty-one?"

One thirty-one was Mileski and his partner, Hiram Quail. Suze and Norm heard Mileski's voice come back, "Thirty-one."

"I've got a car parked on a fire hydrant at 210 W. Grand."

"Ten-four, squad."

A new voice. "One twenty-seven."

"Twenty-seven. Go."

"I need an RD number for an attempted strongarm robbery."

"Uh—your number's gonna be 660932."

"Thanks much."

Norm and Suze rolled south on Wells, Norm driving and Suze doing a good eyeballing of the street. This part of Wells was a patchwork retail mix of run-down cigar and miscellany stores, trendy boutiques, newsstands that specialized in stroke magazines, cheap shoe stores, a Ripley's Believe It or Not Museum, coffee shops with early-bird special dinners and upscale yuppie restaurants where you could pay fifty bucks for a hundred calories. Four black teenagers, three of them boys with Gumby haircuts and one leotard-clad girl, cutting school and throwing shots at each other, lingered around a newsstand. They glanced at the squad car and looked away. A skinny white guy with a wispy beard passed them, cowboy-walking. "One of our known felons," Norm said.

"Brace him?" Suze said.

"He's not breakin' a law."

"Not right *now*."

"Be mellow, my man."

Coming the other way were two women in high heels, wearing fur coats that were hardly necessary, given the mild weather, the coats open in front, heavy gold chains swinging, very high heels, and purses dangling by their straps from one hand. Norm slowed. The white guy and the black kids watched the women peck their way along the street.

"Volunteer victims," Norm said.

The radio said, "Twenty-seven, your VIN is coming back clear."

"Ten-four."

"Thirty-one?"

"Thirty-one."

"We got a maroon Chevy blew the stoplight at—"

Norm shrugged as the women achieved the next block unharmed. He accelerated away from the curb. The radio said, "One thirty-three."

Suze picked up the mike. "Thirty-three."

"We got a shoplifting, Sounds of the Times, 279 Wells, two male whites, fifteen to eighteen years old."

"Somebody holding them?" Suze said.

"Nope. Fled on foot, knocked over an old man. Check on the man, plus see the manager. Mr. Stone."

The address was a block north of their car's beat boundary, but thirty-one was tied up, so it was reasonable for them to slide on over.

Sounds of the Times was one of the seriously trendy ones. The double window display, with glossy chrome-and-ebony frames around the windows and the entry between them, was laid out on sheets of casually rumpled blue denim. "Dance through the Decades" was spelled out in letters cut from sheet music that hung from barely visible threads above the display. There were rows of CDs, and beneath them rows of shoes of the period when the music was popular, starting in the left window with the 1890s, Strauss waltzes and kid pumps with little seed pearls, through Cuban heels and Friml with a gap where a CD had been taken out, and Billy Rose with T-strap dancing shoes, through the early fifties, saddle shoes then penny loafers and Nat "King" Cole. In the right window the late fifties segued into Elvis and then the Beatles, with strap sandals, then Earth shoes, and acid rock, up to 2 Live Crew, and MC Hammer and in front of these a pair of inflatable Reeboks. A pretty nice window, Figueroa thought, although it would have been nicer-looking if the display hadn't been in such rigid rows.

The old man sat on a bench outside the store, trembling. Like many old men, his face looked like a peach—a three-day growth of soft white beard against an old pink skin. He was dressed in an aged windbreaker. He looked bitterly cold, despite the pleasant weather.

"See if he's hurt. I'll check with the manager," Norm said. The manager was striding toward the front door already. He wore a white shirt with navy and red sleeve garters and a navy vest and pants.

Suze sat down on the bench. "You okay?" she asked.

"I guess."

"What's your name, sir?"

"Minton. Raymond Minton."

"What happened to you, Mr. Minton?"

"Um—" He shook his head as if he wasn't sure.

"How old are you, Mr. Minton?"

"Eighty-seven," he said with some pride and complete clarity.

"And where do you live?"

"Fassbinder House."

Something less than a nursing home, more than a residence hotel. Figueroa knew it. Supervised living it was called, for the indigent elderly. About a block and a half west of here. She had been inside with a walkaway a couple of weeks before. It was functional.

Minton's head bobbed up and down on a skinny neck. The hair was thin and white on top of his head and hadn't been cut recently. Wisps of it moved in the breeze. The man needed a hat, Suze Figueroa thought. A wool hat.

"What happened here?" she said.

"Pushed me down." He was, sadly, not at all amazed. It had probably happened before.

"How? Where?"

"I was going out of the store. Under that alarm arch thing. One of 'em was just ahead of me. The other one was coming through and gave me a shove. Pushed me right down. Like I was—a door or something like that in his way. Just shoved me away. And then the alarm went off."

"You fell?"

"Mmm-mm." He pointed at his knee. The pants leg was roughed and a little blood soaked into the fabric from underneath. Thin blood, Figueroa thought.

"Can you stand on it?"

"Oh sure!" he said and got up to show her. He sat down immediately, a little sheepish at his weakness. But not as if anything was broken, Suze thought with some relief. The

125

hand that lay in his lap was skinned on the palm and the ball of the thumb was bleeding. Caught himself on the hand and knee. Better that than break an elbow. She'd had one of them last week, and he'd screamed so much she could hardly hear the dispatcher to call for an ambulance.

"Wait here, please, Mr. Minton."

Bennis had got the manager calmed down. It wasn't that the guy was scared. Mr. Stone was angry, bright red in the face.

"Slouching around the store! I gotta keep my eyes on all of 'em at once!" he said. "I hate kids. Punks!"

"I guess *mosta* your customers are kids, though, huh?" Bennis said.

"Shit! Yeah!"

Bennis sighed; his mild suggestion that the store profited from teenagers had done nothing to honey up Mr. Stone. "So let me get a description."

"Punks!"

"Yeah, I know. Black punks or white punks?"

"I told you guys that when I called in!"

"Tell me again."

"White, and by the way—"

"Height?"

"Medium. Like five ten. One was maybe a little shorter than that."

"Weight?"

"Skinny. Both of 'em. Brown hair. And skinheads."

"Skinheads! Really?" Chicago didn't have many skinheads. Yet. Let's keep our fingers crossed, Bennis thought.

"Well, not *real* skinheads, but their hair was cut right to the scalp up to here," he said, indicating an inch above the tops of his ears. "I hate that bald haircut they wear."

"Eye color?"

"Hey! How'm I gonna see a thing like that? Sneaky little monsters keep their eyes squinted anyhow!"

Bennis said, "Clothes?"

"Black leather jackets, running shoes, Levi's. Jackets must've cost more than I make a *week*."

At the clothing description, which narrowed it to maybe eighty percent of the teenagers in the city, Bennis sighed again, loud enough for Stone to hear him and frown. "Distinguishing features?"

"Ugly bastards. One was pimply. Other one was trying to grow a mustache. Hah! Smirking at me with five hairs on his upper lip!"

Bennis got on the radio and put out the description. Figueroa sidled over to the window displays. She looked at the gap.

"See which way they went?" Bennis asked Stone.

"Nah. Right into the crowd out there and zip!"

"Mr. Minton," Figueroa said, walking out the door, "did *you* see which way they went?"

"There." Minton pointed south.

"Fled southbound," Bennis said. "Mr. Stone?"

"Yeah?"

"How many CDs did they have on 'em when they took off?"

"How do I know? Didn't even know there was a problem until the door alarm went off. There's the one missin' outa the window, but probably they loaded up before they boogied. Shit! Anyhow, by the time the alarm goes off they're outa here. Fat lot of good the alarm is. And that old guy's lyin' on the sidewalk. You don't think he's gonna sue us, do ya? The old guy?"

"I wouldn't know, Mr. Stone."

"Better not. His own fault, gettin' in the way."

Figueroa strolled around while Bennis told the dispatcher that the teens could have one or more stolen CDs on them.

"Never catch 'em now," Stone said. "Took you guys five minutes to get here."

"Two," Bennis said. "You called at 3:11. We rolled up at 3:13."

"Well, it's five minutes *now*. They could be anywhere."

Bennis shrugged. Too true.

Outside, Figueroa sat down on the bench next to the old man. "How's that knee now, Mr. Minton?" she said.

"Don't know." He stretched the leg out. The thin fabric of his worn pants pulled back from the blood-stained knee and he winced. He dragged his pants leg up a few inches with one blue-veined hand, picking the fabric loose from the skin. His shinbone looked sharp above the sagging sock.

"Are you married, Mr. Minton?" Figueroa said.

"Was. Her name was Helen. She's dead."

"How long have you been living at Fassbinder House?"

"Four years."

"How do you like it? Pretty Spartan?" For a second she wondered if he'd know what Spartan meant. Or would remember if he had once known. When he answered, she felt as chagrined as if she had been visibly condescending.

"It isn't bad. The food's warm."

And how basic that was, Figueroa thought.

"Mr. Minton, I guess you and your wife used to dance," Figueroa said. "To Friml."

He didn't answer.

"Do they have a CD player at the Fassbinder?"

He didn't answer.

"What do they play on it?"

The old man groaned. "Show tunes," he said. "Broadway

shows. From the Forties and Fifties."

"I see."

"Do you? They think—the nice children who run the Fassbinder think—we were young in the Forties and Fifties. They can't imagine anybody being older than that. Young! I was forty-seven in 1950!" He started to laugh, laughed and laughed, showing missing teeth and an old tongue, creased and bluish-pink, laughed until he started to cough. But he caught himself then and quieted.

Figueroa said, "I'll tell the manager it was a mistake."

"Fourteen dollars for one disc!" he said. It could have been fourteen thousand.

"Give it to me, Mr. Minton, and I'll take it back."

He grabbed her arm in a bony grip. "I wouldn't have said the kids did it. I really wouldn't have. If they hadn't pushed me."

Bennis said, "How'd you know?"

"With a missing Friml? Kids these days aren't into that."

"Some could be, Suze my man."

"The kind wearing that sort of outfit? That kind of haircut?"

"Not likely."

"Scholarly types maybe. Plus, these kids were out of here by 3:11."

"So?"

"School's out at 3:30. They were cutting school. These are not your scholars, Bennis. If MC Hammer had been lifted, okay. But Rudolf Friml?"

Bennis nodded. They got back in the squad car.

"He gonna just skate, Figueroa?"

"Yeah, I cut him loose."

"Um—"

"Hey, Bennis, you figure he's gonna go on to a life of crime? He's eighty-seven years old."

"How we gonna put it down?"

"Unfounded."

"Okay."

"What's the matter?"

"I saw you buy the CD from Stone. For the old guy."

"Shit, don't look at me like that. I saved us two hours in the district handling the paper."

"Figueroa, my man, climb down. You are preaching to the converted. I already called in for fifteen minutes' personal time. I'm gonna buy you a cup of coffee."

"Why me?"

"I figure it'll take you that long to get over bein' human."

"See No Evil" is the first time Cat Marsala ever appeared in a short story. A situation exactly like this actually happened in Chicago. A police officer, a friend of a friend, had been accused of a "bad shooting." I enjoy reading autopsy reports and, looking his case over, realized what had happened. This story is fiction, but only a degree removed from reality.

See No Evil

"I hate mysteries. This kind anyway," Harold McCoo said. He pushed his swivel chair around to hand me my cup of coffee.

"Mysterious coffee?"

"Oh, hell, no. It's Sulawesi Kalosi. Aromatic with a gently woody undertone. Javanese type."

"What, then?"

McCoo is Chief of Detectives, Department of Police, City of Chicago. He didn't get to that position by wasting a lot of time. He shoved a large pile of paper toward me. "I want a favor, Cat."

"Anything for you."

"An investigation. And we're going to cut you loose some money for it, too."

"You don't have to—"

"Yeah, I do. I want you official. You're gonna need to see confidential documents. So confidential that even the subject, Officer Bennis, isn't allowed to see them."

"Documents about what?"

He sipped his coffee. McCoo makes very good coffee.

"You know, Cat, people don't change. We've got lemons in the department, Piltdown men, but they show up pretty soon. You take an officer like Bennis, eleven years on the job, not one problem. He was in Six for eight years. His commander there has nothing but praise for him. He's been in One for three years now, and even though Commander Coumadin's an idiot, he admits Bennis has been professional, no whiff of brutality. He's been a street officer all that time, not a desk man. He's not going to suddenly up and *execute* somebody."

"I suppose not. I take it somebody thinks he did. Was there some sort of danger—?"

"He thought the guy had killed his partner."

"That's a reason."

"Not much of one. Somebody who's been on the street eleven years—he's been in tight places before, and he's had threats against his partner before, and a zillion times he's been scared. It's that kind of job."

"Okay. That makes sense."

"But they're going to destroy him. The Office of Professional Standards is gonna make an example of him. When the complaint is sustained, they'll suspend him. And there's a rumor they're thinking criminal prosecution."

There had been a lot of talk in the Chicago media that OPS didn't often sustain brutality complaints. The process for investigating complaints, they said, was a washing machine: stuff went in dirty and came out clean. There was some truth to that, too, but much more in the past than now.

"And this Bennis—"

"Isn't the kind to do something like this. But it looks like he did. And the OPS investigator, Hulce, is out to get him. The hell of it is, his story has holes."

"Bennis is a patrol officer? You're Chief of Detectives. Why is it your problem?"

"The detectives do the initial investigation."

"And?"

"Ah, I know the kid slightly."

"Oh, really?"

"I knew his mother, once upon a time. What we need, Cat, is a fresh eye on it."

"I don't do whitewashes."

"Hey, I'm not asking for a spin doctor. I need a private eye. There's something wrong someplace and a good guy is gonna suffer. I don't have the time to deal with it, and everybody here is either strongly pro or strongly con, both of which I don't want. I want you to look at the papers without me giving you any predigested ideas. Here." He patted the stack of paper. "You figure it out."

"Oh, well. If you've got the money, honey, I've got the time."

The Furlough bar was never going to be a photo opportunity for *Architectural Digest*. There were no ferns, no hanging plants, nothing green and growing in the whole place, unless there was something alive under the slatted floor at the beer taps that nobody knew about. The front window hadn't been washed since Eisenhower was president and was now a uniform, suede-finish gray, about the texture of peach skin. Thirty years earlier Royal Crown cola had given out signs for doors with little slots where the proprietor could insert the times the place was open. The Furlough's hadn't been replaced since it was first attached; several numbers had fallen sideways and some had fallen off, so the sign now read that the bar was open Thursdays from   :00 to ∞.

The Furlough was owned by two retired cops and was diagonally across the street from the Chicago Police Department's central headquarters at Eleventh and State. I was supposed to meet my people at the bar at three-thirty p.m. They would have just got off an eight-hour tour.

When I walked in, I could feel emotion in the air. It wasn't me, wasn't because a female had walked in. There were a couple of women cops in the bar already. The tension was there before I arrived. I could see it in the spacing of the people around the bar. My two cops, whose pictures I had seen in the Chief of Detectives' office, were sitting alone at the far end of the zinc bar. One was Officer Susannah Maria Figueroa, a short, young white woman. Sitting next to her was her partner Norm Bennis, a stocky black man of about thirty-five, ten years older than Figueroa. His head was down between his shoulders. Then there was a gap of four stools, followed by two white men, one tall and one pudgy with a shiny pink face, a black woman whose elbow leaned on the bar and whose hand cupped her chin, and another, older white man next to her.

The bunch of four were carefully not looking at Figueroa and her partner.

I walked over to her. In these situations, I make as much effort as possible to look like a fellow cop. I'm not; ordinarily I make my living as a reporter. Generally speaking, cops don't love reporters.

I said, "Hi, I'm Cat Marsala."

They looked at me with a total lack of enthusiasm, the way you might look at a parking ticket on your windshield.

But they had orders from the Chief of Detectives. Figueroa said, "I'm Suze Figueroa. This is my partner, Norm Bennis."

He extended his hand. If Figueroa looked glum, Bennis was sunk in an abyss of gloom. But his face had laugh lines. Which currently were not being used.

I shook his hand.

"Let's go over there," Figueroa said. There were three

tables in the place. Their tops were about as big as lids from Crisco cans. If all three of us wanted to put our elbows on the table, there wouldn't be room.

"What's the matter with these other guys?" I mumbled to Figueroa, cutting my eyes toward the four at the bar. "They mad at you for something?"

"Trying to cheer us up," Figueroa said.

"So I yelled at 'em," Bennis said.

"Oh." I waited, but neither spoke. "All right, you two. You know why I'm here."

"Because I killed a guy," Bennis said.

He took a break then, bringing back three beers. I wanted to hear the story from them before I read the documents, but I didn't want to be jacked around all afternoon, either. I said, "Talk!"

Bennis shrugged. "I don't see what you can do about it."

"Humor me."

He said, "Okay, okay. We're on second watch. It's about two in the afternoon, Saturday, we're in the car we usually get and we're maybe an hour, hour and a half, to the end of the tour. There's an in-progress call. Citizen calls 911, describes it as a rape and he's right. One thirty-one responds. The woman is cut and she's yelling to the car that the asshole has a knife. A second unit, one thirty-six, responds and when they get in sight of the woman, the jerk was taking off. One thirty-one follows him to an apartment building. We hear the radio traffic and get over to the building. Mileski and Quail in one thirty-one have separated. Quail to the back door and Mileski to the front. They've got the place buttoned up, so Suze and I run into the hall. Far as we know the asshole's raping somebody else. There's an apartment door open, and a woman yelling."

"She was saying 'You idiot!' in Spanish," Figueroa said.

"So we go in. Long, dark hall. In the apartment, the

shades are pulled most of the way down, because the woman who lives there is watching soap operas.

"We run in, and the guy's standing in the living room— name's Zeets—and the TV light is glinting off the knife and he says he's gonna kill us. Figueroa draws on him and screams 'Drop the knife!' about yea zillion times. So do I. Finally the asshole throws the knife on a chair. I've got my service revolver out by now and I hold it on him while Figueroa starts to cuff him, except I can't see hardly at all because the light from the windows, what there is of it, is behind them.

"Then, like in a split second, he whips around with one cuff on and grabs Figueroa's gun and they lurch back away from me. They're wrestling for the gun. I know it, but I'm supposed to stay back and take aim, which I do, but I can't see much. It's too dark. They're wrestling back and forth and then there's a shot. I figure Figueroa's been shot.

"I can't see who's got the gun, and they're still struggling, but I can see the guy's outline and I fire at him." He stopped a second and looked at me doubtfully. "You know that if we fire at all, we're supposed to try to kill him? I mean no winging him in the hand, that cowboy kind of stuff."

"I know."

"I fire six times. He drops." Bennis ducked his head. "Basically, he's dead."

"So. I don't see what's wrong."

"His mother and two sisters were in the apartment. They're saying I didn't need to shoot him. They're saying it was obvious that Figueroa had the gun. All three of 'em."

"Oh."

"I'm gonna be suspended or fired. Probably fired. And they're talking about prosecution for manslaughter."

"I understand. That's scary."

"No you don't."

I never like it when people say I don't understand something. Personally, I think I'm pretty sympathetic. But Bennis
was so upset, I forgave him. "So tell me."

"It's not the manslaughter thing. I love this job."

His voice was filled with frustration and anger. Bennis and
Figueroa seemed to have relaxed their initial distrust of me
somewhat. I asked Figueroa, "Is that what happened? What
Bennis says?"

"Yeah. Zeets and I both had hold of the gun when it went
off. Thank God it was pointed up. Went into the ceiling."

"So you back up Bennis?"

"Totally." She punched Bennis's shoulder lightly. "This
is a good man." For just a second real affection came over her
face. "All he wanted to do was save my life."

The mutual trust in their relationship was obvious. Out in
the street, alone, in danger, in the dark—sure, two cops had
to trust each other. It was horrible when an officer was paired
with somebody he couldn't rely on. In this case, clearly, they
leaned on each other every time they hit the streets and neither had let the other down.

Rising, I said, "All right. I'll be getting back to you."

As we moved to the door, the pink-faced officer at the bar
said, "Hey! You gonna help Bennis?"

"I hope I—"

The woman officer said, "They're gonna railroad our
buddy."

Another cop said, "OPS ain't any better than civilians."

"Yeah, your basic citizen'll turn on you in two seconds
flat!"

"They see a mugger you're their best friend."

"Hear a noise in the night—"

"Teenagers *congregatin'*—"

"Guys passin' around little bags of white stuff—"

"But you grab the mugger and next thing they're screamin' police brutality."

"I ever tell you about the time I chased these two guys down the alley off Van Buren near Plymouth Court?"

Suze said, "Yeah, Mileski, you did."

"*She* didn't hear it," he said, pointing to me.

"She doesn't want to, either."

"Three a.m. and not one breathing soul around. Responded to an alarm at a jewelry store. Two guys they're sharing about one neuron in their heads between the two of 'em, but one of 'em had a sawed-off shotgun."

"Very illegal!" the woman cop said.

"Guy takes a shot at me, misses, and they both run. I'm in pursuit. My hat flies off, I'm outta breath, but I manage to hang on ta my radio. Run 'em down after six blocks. The jerk with the gun falls over a gas can somebody threw out, loses the gun, I cuff him, pick up the shotgun in one hand, got my service revolver in the other—we're talking two-gun Pete here—aim 'em both at the other guy, who's too fat to climb over the fence and escape, and the guy gets so scared he starts to cry."

He stopped and looked at me. "Well, great!" I said, wondering what he was getting at.

"Brought 'em both in. Single-handed. Know what happened to me? No department commendation. No nothing!"

"That's too bad."

"But!" He said it again, "But! *But!* They gammee a fine for losing my cap!"

"Oh."

"That's nice, Mileski," Bennis said. "But we're trying to have a private conversation here now."

"Oh, well, excuuuuse me."

However, there really wasn't much else to say. I nodded to

them and said, "I've got the papers. I'll be in touch."

I thought I'd been encouraging, but apparently the sight of me had not made Bennis think he was saved. As I went out past the ancient bar sign, he said softly to Figueroa, "It's hopeless."

Armed with nine pounds of CPD paperwork, twelve ounces of coffee, and a half-pound bar of chocolate, I settled in at home for a good read.

There were sixty pages of photocopied photos alone: crime scene photos, autopsy photos, and spent pellet photos. Typed statements from the mother and both sisters, headed OFFICE OF PROFESSIONAL STANDARDS, the interviewer being the OPS investigator C. Hulce. A transcript of the radio activity that afternoon. Typed statements from Figueroa and Bennis, also interviewed by C. Hulce. Interviews with Mileski and Quail. An interview with the rape victim whose case had started all this off. A plat of the apartment, with the position of the body. Another plat of the apartment with the position of the officers at the time of the shooting. Copies of the hospital reports, labeled "Emergency Room Outpatient Report"—Figueroa had been cut on the jaw during the scuffle by the barrel of her own gun. Releases allowing the hospital to give the reports to the OPS. Consent forms. A dozen Shooting Investigation Reports. Disciplinary Action forms. A fifty-page document called "Summary to the Commanding Officer." Something called a Weapon Discharge Report. Evidence lists. Diagrams showing the position of the wounds on the body. Autopsy protocol from the pathologist, addressed "Cook County Institute of Forensic Medicine." Inventory of the officers' weapons. Ballistics tests. One sheet from ballistics stated that the bullet reclaimed from the ceiling matched Figueroa's gun. A Waiver of Counsel/

Request to Secure Counsel. Both Bennis and Figueroa, who was not charged but was questioned, requested counsel. And about a hundred one-page things headed "Supplementary Report."

An army may travel on its stomach, but a police department travels on its paperwork.

One printed sheet advised the officer of his or her rights. While they could have counsel, as far as the department was concerned, that was about all they got. They had no right to remain silent. If they remained silent, they would be "ordered by a superior officer to answer the question." If they persisted in refusing to answer, they were advised that "such refusal constitutes a violation of the Rules and Regulations of the Chicago Police Department and will serve as a basis for which your discharge will be sought."

I suppose it is a privilege, not a right, to remain a police officer. And I suppose they need to be able to get rid of the crazies, but it certainly had Bennis pinned down so that he had to answer them. And he seemed to have made some mistakes.

There was a sheet of charges. Boiled down, he was accused of (1) discharging a firearm without justification, and (2) failing to give a true and accurate account of the incident relative to the shooting of Jorge Sanabria.

His primary accuser was the dead man's mother.

OFFICE OF PROFESSIONAL STANDARDS

26 Mar 93

CR #9956291

Statement of witness, Benicia Sanabria, relative to the incident that led to the death of Jorge (Zeets) Sanabria on 12 Mar 93 at 1400 hours.

Statement taken at 1121 S. State, Chicago IL 60607

Questioned by:	Inv. C. Hulce, Star 337, Unit 243
Date & Time:	26 Mar 1993 at 1320 hours.
Witnessed by:	Inv. Clarence Summerset, Star 633, Unit 243

Hulce: What is your full name, address, and telephone number?

Sanabria: Benicia Sanabria, 731 W. Sangin, 312/555-8997.

Hulce: What is your marital status?

Sanabria: I am a widow.

Hulce: Are you giving this statement of your own free will, without the promise of exoneration or reward of any nature being given to you?

Sanabria: Yes.

Hulce: Do you work? If so, give the name of the company, address, telephone number, and length of employment.

My eye skimmed down the page to:

Hulce: What is the relationship of Jorge Sanabria to you?

Sanabria: He is my only son.

Hulce: What occurred on 12 March 1993 about 1400 hours at your home that resulted in the death of Jorge "Zeets" Sanabria?

Sanabria: I was home. I work Sunday through Thursday. Suddenly Jorge came running in.

Hulce: Was he carrying anything?

Sanabria: He was. Well, yes, he was. It was a knife.

Hulce: What happened then?

Sanabria: Then, well, then he said, "They're after me," and my daughter said—um, she called him a name and

141

she said, "What did you do?" and he started swearing. And my daughter said something about Jorge disgracing her and then a police officer came into the front of the hall. The door, our door to the hall, was still open, and the man said, "Police officer, come out!" or something like that. But he stayed in the hall and then two other police officers came in. And Jorge backed into the living room.

Hulce: Describe them, please.

Sanabria: One was a woman. She was short and dark-haired and I think she was possibly Chicana. The other was a black man. Taller but not tall.

Hulce: What happened then?

Sanabria: Then they all yelled, "Put the knife down!" But Jorge didn't.

Hulce: Did he say anything to the officers?

Sanabria: He said words I will not repeat. But that's no reason to shoot him dead.

Hulce: Then what happened?

Sanabria: They said to get back, so I am standing in the doorway to the living room. I can see in at an angle, so I do not see the man well, but the woman and Jorge. Jorge threw the knife on the chair. The woman put one handcuff on Jorge. Then he threw her back and grabbed her gun. And they struggled for the gun. He should not have done this, but that's no reason to shoot him dead.

Hulce: Then what happened?

Sanabria: The gun went off. The woman had pointed it at the ceiling, and then Jorge lost hold of it. Then the man shot him dead.

Hulce: After the woman officer had regained possession of the gun?

Sanabria: Yes, after. Two, three seconds after. And I shouted, "Stop, you are killing him." But he did not stop.

Hulce: Was it bright enough to see?

Sanabria: Oh, yes. Very bright enough. The shades were pulled down, but not all the way. And, the television was on. It gives light. Off and on. Depending on—how do I say this?—whether the behind part of the picture—I know, the background—whether it is bright. You could see just fine.

Hulce: After reading this statement and finding it to be what you said, will you sign it?

Sanabria: Yes.

Both Sanabria sisters confirmed what their mother said. The younger girl, however, had been in the kitchen throughout the event, and could only report what she heard. Both girls were well spoken and specific, although the older one had some angry comments about the police.

Then there was Bennis's side:

OFFICE OF PROFESSIONAL STANDARDS

26 Mar. 1993

Statement of accused, Officer Norman Bennis, star 31992, Unit 001, relative to allegations that on 12 March 1993 at approximately 1400 hours, inside a first-floor apartment at 731 W. Sangin he discharged his firearm without justification, resulting in the death of Jorge Sanabria. It is further alleged that he failed to give a true and accurate account of the incident relative to the shooting of Jorge Sanabria.

Statement being taken at the Office of Professional Standards, 1024 S. Wabash, Chicago IL 60605.

Questioned and typed by:	Inv. C. Hulce, Star 337, Unit 243
Date & Time:	24 Mar. 1993 at 1335 hours.
Witnessed by:	Attorney Frederick Melman FOP
	1300 E. Chicago Ave. Chicago IL 60611
	Inv. Clarence Summerset, Star 633, Unit 243

Bennis prefaced his remarks with the formula the FOP counsel would have given him. And both he and C. Hulce seemed to have fallen victim to creeping officialese.

Bennis: I want to say that I am not giving this statement voluntarily, but under duress. I am giving this statement because I have been advised by the Police Department regulations that if I do not I will be fired from my job.

Hulce: Relate what happened on 12 March 93 at 1400 hours in the apartment at 731 W. Sangin that resulted in the death of Jorge "Zeets" Sanabria.

Bennis: I ran in past Officer Mileski, who was guarding the front door so as Zeets wouldn't escape. My partner, Officer Figueroa, was ahead of me. A woman was in the doorway of the apartment screaming at Zeets. He was brandishing a weapon, a knife with a six-inch blade. I said drop the knife. He backed into a dark room and Figueroa and I followed. We had our guns drawn. Figueroa said drop the knife. The room was very dark. After being cautioned many times, he threw the knife onto a yellow and pink flowered chair.

Figueroa began to cuff him. Then he suddenly threw her off and he jumped her and they were struggling. Her gun went off. I could not see well because of the lack of light, but when I saw a silhouette which I knew to be Zeets and not my partner, even though they were close together, I fired. Fearing for my life and for the life of my partner, I discharged my weapon six times.

Hulce: Then what happened?

Bennis: Then the woman I now know to be Mrs. Sanabria ran in and she said you've killed my son, and the woman I now know to be Anne Sanabria started to hit me . . .

That was about it. I flipped pages until I found Suze Figueroa's statement. It was almost exactly like Bennis's. Not so much alike that I thought they had rehearsed all their answers with each other, but they certainly had talked it over. Still—that was natural, under the circumstances. Figueroa's statement added one detail. She said that at the instant when her gun went off, she and Zeets each had one hand on it, because Zeets had pulled her other hand away, and it was Zeets pulling the trigger that actually caused the discharge. Then his hand came off the gun. But because of the darkness she was certain Bennis couldn't see Zeets's hand had left the gun.

A sheet headed FINAL INCIDENT REPORT/RECOMMENDATION OF INVESTIGATOR, written by C. Hulce, OPS investigator, concluded that Bennis did not have to shoot, that the incident was over and Figueroa had regained control of her gun before Bennis started firing, that he could see well enough to know that the danger was past, since he had been able to describe the pink and yellow flowered chair. The light level had been confirmed by the Sanabrias, Hulce added, and Bennis, therefore, had not only fired without justification, but had lied in telling the investigators that he could not see. "Since Officer Bennis was able to describe the chair both in pattern and color, it is unreasonable to claim that he could not see the victim and the other officer."

Hulce believed that Figueroa had also lied in saying Bennis couldn't see Zeets's hand was off the gun, but they apparently weren't pushing a charge against her.

Unspoken was Bennis's motive. That he had been enraged at the attack on Figueroa—which certainly was life-threatening for a few seconds—and had killed Zeets intentionally.

An idea of what had really happened was taking shape in my head. Looking through the hefty pile of documents, I finally found the transcript of the radio traffic. I read it three times. It confirmed my theory. What I needed now was to hear the actual radio transmission, live, as it happened that day. No problem. McCoo could set that up. If I called him first thing in the morning, we'd probably be able to hear it in the afternoon.

I met Figueroa and Bennis in the anteroom on the fifth floor. The windows looked over Chicago to the west. Somewhere out there a dusky feather of smoke rose from a fire. Bennis's arms hung drearily at his sides and his eyes were half-closed. He flopped into a plastic chair.

"What do you know about the Sanabrias?" I asked them. "Can you claim they aren't reliable witnesses? They certainly have reason to be biased."

Suze looked at Norm. "They—yes, I suppose. Zeets, you know, had been dealing drugs for years."

I said, "I hear some hesitation in your voice."

"Well, it's the old story. The wild son, two hard-working daughters. Zeets has a long sheet for attacking women. The mother is a good person. Very nice. She works washing and packaging vegetables in a supermarket. The older daughter is a stockbroker. The younger daughter's still in high school. She's an honor student—"

"And?"

"I don't feel very comfortable characterizing them as petty crooks who'd swear to anything."

I watched Norm as he rose suddenly and went to stand next to the window. The shade fabric was yellow and cast a mustard glow on his face. I said to her again, "And?"

"And these are—jeez, these are my people. In some sense, I'm not very comfortable with the, you know, putting the image on them. The image of the sleazy Hispanic."

Norm said, "Shit!"

Then we got word to go into the hearing room.

Investigator C. Hulce, Office of Professional Standards, turned out to be Corinne Hulce. She was a short woman with strong shoulders and a hungry mouth—a jackal of a woman. McCoo sat next to her, wearing his indulgent face. Also in McCoo's office were Commander Coumadin, Bennis's commander in the First District, and Melman, the attorney retained for Bennis by the Fraternal Order of Police.

We went through the introductions in a spirit of great caution on everybody's part.

Then Coumadin said, "Play the tape. That's what we're here for."

I had read the transcription, but hearing it was very different. Even though it was only voices, all the urgency was there. I could imagine the tension in the Communications Room, as well as on the street, as the incident developed.

The dispatcher said, "One thirty-one," which meant beat car thirty-one in the First District.

Officer Quail said, "Thirty-one."

"I have a woman screaming for help at 110 West Adams."

"Ten-four," he said, acknowledging the call and also by code that he was in a two-man car.

"Thirty-three," said the voice of a woman officer.

"Go ahead, one thirty-three."

"That alarm you gave me? The manager says it's gone off four times this week. Plus, there was a runner there. The call you had said no runner."

"Thanks, thirty-three. We'll get onto it." It was important for alarm companies to tell the police when they were sending runners. Otherwise, a cop coming on the call could think the runner was the burglar. "While you're there, thirty-three, we have three teenagers beating up a man at State and Jackson. Citizen called it in."

"Ten-ninety-nine, squad."

"I didn't know you were a ninety-nine unit," the dispatcher said. Ninety-nine meant a one-man car. "Let me know if you need backup."

"Will do."

Quail's voice said, "Thirty-one."

"Go ahead, thirty-one."

"We have an attempted rape here! We need a unit to take the woman for medical attention. Subject took off westbound."

"Okay. Uh—one thirty-six?"

"Thirty-six."

"See the woman at 110 West Adams."

"Ninety-nine."

"Do you have a description, thirty-one?"

"Yeah, uh, male white Hispanic, twenty years old, black hair, light complexion, wearing black Reeboks, black shirt, Levi's." This was a description that would distinguish him from at best half the young adult males on the street.

Quail's voice said, "Squad, thirty-six is here. We're in pursuit."

"Other units, the suspect is . . ."

The dispatcher repeated the description. Half a minute passed. Some officer said, "Hezz foggl ztt!" the transmission garbled. There was a series of gasps, as if somebody was running and trying to talk at the same time, then, "—any other units he's dangerous!" Then, "We got him! He's going into a building at 731 West Sangin."

The dispatcher said calmly, "Twenty-seven? You in the area? Can you back up thirty-one?"

Norm Bennis's voice said, "Ten-four. We're three blocks away, westbound on Jackson."

There was another half minute or so without any transmissions. This was the period, I knew, when Suze and Norm pulled up in front of the building on Sangin. They found that the two officers in thirty-one had split up, one to guard the back door and one in the front hall.

Bennis's voice again: "One twenty-seven."

"Go ahead, twenty-seven."

"Thirty-one has the suspect isolated in a first-floor apartment. He's supposed to have a knife."

At the same time, the dispatcher was saying, "Anybody in the vicinity?"

"Twenty-nine. I'm at Monroe and Michigan. I'll roll on over."

There was a short period of silence. Then Bennis said, "Twenty-seven."

"Twenty-seven, go."

"We probably got enough units. They have him bottled up at 731 West Sangin, and we're going in, squad. One of the neighbors says he ran in carrying a knife and screaming."

"Twenty-seven's giving a slowdown," the dispatcher said,

conscious that every unit in the area would be wanting to give chase.

A few seconds of buzzing, somebody with an open key on his radio, then Suze's voice: "We have the suspect in an apartment at—hey!"

A new voice screamed, "Always after me!!!"

Suze yelled, "Drop the knife! Drop the knife!"

"Put down the knife!" It was Norm's voice.

Suze: "Put down the knife!"

"Drop it!"

"Drop it! Drop it!! Right now!"

"Yeee—"

"Down!"

"Cuff him!"

"Hands behind your back!"

"Bastards!" This was the unknown voice.

"Ten-one! Ten-one!" somebody said. It sounded like Bennis, but high-pitched. Ten-one means officer in trouble.

The dispatcher started to say, "Units in one, we need backup at 731 West Sangin," but the other noises overrode. We all knew that every unit in the area would be screaming to a halt and turning toward the incident.

"Shit! Goddamn!"

Dispatcher: "All units stay off the air. One twenty-seven has an emergency."

"Hey! Back off!"

A shot. That would have been Suze's gun.

"Shit! Ahhh! Shit!"

There were two shots. Then one shot. Then two or three more, fast. Then there was a sound like metal scraping on a sidewalk, but so unnerving that I thought it was actually a human voice, screaming.

"He's hit!" somebody said.

Immediately Bennis's voice said, "Twenty-seven. We need an ambulance here." His voice wasn't panicky, but it was tight as a guitar string.

The dispatcher said, "Fire's rolling, twenty-seven."

"Right," I said to Commander Coumadin. "That makes everything clear."

"What?" He realized this was not a commanderlike answer, so he said, "In what way, Ms. Marsala?"

"Norm was right. He was telling the truth. And so was the family. They were both telling the truth. The family and your officers."

"But they disagree."

"They disagree and they're both right. They were both telling the truth."

Investigator Hulce snapped, "That's not possible."

"Suppose I show you that it is. What happens?"

"We—well, of course we'd drop the charges."

"And clean up Bennis's record?"

"Certainly," she said huffily, not believing me. "Play the tape again."

Hulce rewound the tape after a nod from the commander. I said, "You have a synchronous tape that tells the time this was recorded, right?"

Hulce said, "Right."

"Stop and mark when I tell you." Hulce glanced at the brass, hoping they'd slap me down for giving her orders, but they didn't. The tape began to play.

The dispatcher said, "We have a woman screaming for help at—"

We listened as three minutes passed. Then, Norm Bennis's voice said, "They have him bottled up at 731 West Sangin, and we're going in, squad."

I said, "Mark tape." Hulce punched a button and a different voice said, "Fourteen oh-three hours, fifteen seconds."

The drama unfolded again, unseen, with the strange, occasional sounds from radios where the key was briefly opened, like flashes of light in darkness. We heard the commands to drop the knife. We heard the shots. I said, "Now!"

"Fourteen oh-three hours, fifty-seven seconds."

"Only forty-two seconds!" Suze said.

I said, "Right. Forty-two seconds from the moment Bennis entered the house to the moment he fired."

Bennis said, "It seemed like five minutes."

"To you. But not in terms of the actions you described. Everything happened very, very fast."

"He's not going to get off because of *that*," Hulce barked. She added sententiously, "An officer has to be able to make split-second decisions."

"That's not what I'm talking about."

Norm Bennis was studying me and finally spoke. "Tell me." And the seriousness of Bennis's situation must have made even Hulce sympathetic for a couple of seconds, because she shut up.

"Bennis really couldn't see. It was too dark. He did the best he could. He and Figueroa had been driving around for more than six hours. They came in from outdoors. His eyes hadn't adjusted to the dimness in the apartment. Mrs. Sanabria and the daughters had been inside all day. To them it was bright enough. Have you ever walked into a dark restaurant from outdoors? You can't see, and you bump into things, but everybody inside is zipping around carrying trays and pouring drinks and doing fine."

"But he told us the exact color of the chair!" Coumadin said.

I made my voice as patient at I could. It wouldn't do Bennis and Figueroa any good to tell their commander he was an idiot. "By the time they were calling for ambulances, Commander, his eyes had adjusted to the dark."

Hulce was fuming. And why not? She wouldn't look good as a result of this; she should have figured it out herself. I fixed her with my sternest look. She should have thought it out thoroughly before putting Norm through hell. Then I turned to the FOP counsel, Melman.

"Ask an eye doctor. You'll get some figures about just how long it takes a thirty-five-year-old human eye to adapt under those circumstances."

He nodded, then smiled and nodded again more briskly.

In the stretching silence, Bennis jumped up, came over with all the laugh lines on his face laughing, pulled me up out of the chair, and kissed me on the forehead.

"Unprofessional behavior!" Suze Figueroa said. "Give that man thirty days!"

The Cat Marsala series was fairly new when I was asked to write about Washington, D.C. and a cat, the furry kind, not Cat. But since I had met my Cat only a couple of years earlier, this seemed to be a good time to find out how she felt about an ethical question, in other words, get to know her better.

Freedom of the Press

I walked into the office of Representative Peggy Nicklis at 1:55, for a two o'clock appointment. Then I stopped and stared.

She saw my face and started to laugh. When she was done chuckling, she said, "You're Cat Marsala?"

"Yup. Thank you for seeing me, Ms. Nicklis."

"And you expected a much grander office." She was still half-laughing.

"Well, I didn't expect—uh—exposed heat pipes, cracked linoleum, a sloping ceiling, two small rooms—I suppose this outer room is for your secretary?—furniture that looks like it was retired from the Library of Congress, and a window the size of the Elvis stamp." In addition there was a slightly off-center bookcase crammed with books, several reasonably adequate bookcases visible in the inner office, some empty cartons, an old desk in the reception room and an old desk in the inner office. Three phones and an answering machine on each desk. Two very large metal wastebaskets. A plush blue cat bed and a litter box in Nicklis's inner office. And a cat. Everything in both offices was tidy; everything was neat and straight and clean, but the place was definitely shabby. Nicklis watched me, smiling.

"It's a matter of seniority. You get better and better offices the longer you're here. Washington is all about how important you are. This is definitely a starter office. Plus, this isn't the only thing," she said. "The nearest bathroom for women is *seven flights* of stairs from here."

"Jeez!"

"And not just seven flights," she giggled, "but down three, then *up* two, then down two."

"They weren't prepared for you women."

"Well, it also makes you feel sorry for two hundred years of secretaries, dashing for the far-off watercloset."

I had recognized her right away, of course, from a zillion photographs and television interviews. So she seemed like an old friend. She acted like one too, showing me into her office and sitting down next to me in a corner where she had two overstuffed chairs. The cat came over, swept its body across my ankle and told me it wanted to be stroked precisely twice. Cats know exactly what they want. After graciously accepting this homage he allowed Peggy to scratch his ear, then he stared at each of us in turn, collecting admiration.

I asked, "Who is Mr. Cat?"

What I thought she said was:

"His name is Mugum."

"Mugum?" I looked at the tawny, lithe cat. He went to his big, plush cushion and lay down. He lifted one hind leg in the air to inspect it. Apparently decided it was an excellent leg. He put it down and rolled onto his back.

"Mugum is a very unusual name."

"It's spelled 'MGM.' Pronounced Mugum. He's named that because he looks like the MGM lion. MGM is a ginger tom, aren't you, baby?"

"Did you get him after you moved here—"

"Oh, Lord, no! I've had him all his life. He's seven now. We've moved to D.C. together, haven't we, tough guy?

MGM goes everywhere with me."

MGM curled up and went to sleep.

Peggy Nicklis was slender, with dark hair cut blunt. An easy-care style. She wore a suit and flat shoes that would be easy to get around in. My mother would have said, "She doesn't do a lot for herself." Peggy also wasn't what United States culture in the waning days of the twentieth century considered especially beautiful.

Peggy Nicklis certainly wasn't the first woman to serve in the House of Representatives, but she was the first from an extremely conservative district just northwest of Chicago. She had received a considerable amount of media attention because she had won without being particularly flashy in her statements or striking-looking in her photographs. The word for Peggy was businesslike, and she had received the trust of the voters, rather than catching their fancy.

Hal Briskman at *Chicago Today* had said to me:

"What we want is a story about how she's settling in, now that she's been in Washington three weeks. Is D.C. intimidating to her? How does she like her office? Are rents breathtakingly expensive? Does she feel like one of the gang yet?"

"That's not very pithy, Hal."

"We don't want pith. Readers are fed up with pith. Don't talk budget deficit with her, Cat. That's not what we want right now. Don't talk health care. Don't talk education priorities. Do a fluff piece."

"Fluff! I don't do fluff."

"Fluff is good for the soul."

"Not this soul. But I *will* do the interview, if you want."

"And do it the way I want. Keep in mind: you play, we pay."

"Oh, very well."

He said he'd pay for the tickets, meals of course, and two

nights at a hotel in D.C., which adds up. And pay for the article, of course. Well, that's the business I'm in. I'm free-lance, which is always a precarious way to live. And while some of the stories I've done have been big, and my byline is noticed by an occasional reader, I'm not famous.

Being famous would be nice.

Peggy answered my questions straightforwardly. "Well, yes. Rent here truly does take your breath away. For what you'd pay in Chicago for a medium-sized apartment with a Lake Michigan view, here you get one and a half rooms looking out at a fire escape and the brick wall of the building next door ten feet away."

"You're saying we aren't really keeping our legislators happy?"

She smiled. "I wouldn't think of saying that. Anyway, I'm planning to spend most of my time here in the office. I go home mainly to sleep. That way I figure I'll earn more time back in Chicago, too. My folks and my friends are there."

"How about new friends here?"

"I'm meeting a few people. It's slow, though."

"You probably don't have much time to socialize. You have a lot of work and catching up to do."

"Yes. Still, there are parties galore. The White House had the so-called freshmen, the new guys, to dinner. That was exciting. I've been to several special-interest dinners, and a Democratic Party bash in honor of the newcomers. A couple of embassies. My father's family is Polish, so I got asked to their embassy party, of course."

Peggy's secretary called back from late lunch, stuck her head in the door and waved. Peggy introduced her as Annie Boyd.

Peggy said to me, "Could we continue this tomorrow?" To

Annie she said, "It was two o'clock Monday and Tuesday, wasn't it?"

In the outer office, Annie nodded her head, yes, it was Monday and Tuesday at two.

The interviewee is always right. I said, "Sure, and thanks." However, it was supposed to be Monday and Tuesday two to three, and this was only two-thirty. Peggy realized that.

"I know we're stopping early. But let me make up for it tomorrow. I'm still backed up with work and I'm barely unpacked."

Well, who could fault a person for that? The last time I moved, it took three months of my life and three years off my life.

Washington was cold but bright Tuesday, and I spent the morning walking. I strolled the Mall, went into the National Air and Space Museum and the National Gallery, and finally walked up Delaware to eat at one of the fast-food places in the underground mall at Union Station. It was truly fast, served coffee in cups as big as soup bowls, and it let me watch the noon news on an overhead TV. There was trouble in the Middle East, fighting in central Europe, and a newsman for United Press International, Lee Chesterton, whom I knew slightly, had driven off the Frederick Douglass Bridge last night and drowned. It was thought alcohol was involved. He was well known here, and it was a big story with a lot of the usual Washington speculation.

After lunch, the Smithsonian beckoned, but a person needs a week to do it justice. No point right now. I strolled through the National Sculpture Garden instead.

A minute or two before the hour, I arrived at Peggy Nicklis's office. Her secretary Annie simply waved me through. No pomp here. Peggy looked tired and the ginger tom was out of sorts too. He hissed at me, then stalked over to the window, jumped up to the ledge and prowled back and forth.

"I heard about Lee Chesterton's accident on the noon news," I told Peggy. "I'd met him a couple of times when he covered a story in Chicago."

"It's a terrible thing to have happened. He was a nice person."

"Yes, terrible. You dated him a couple of times, didn't you?"

She looked up, surprised. "Two or three times. How did you know that?"

"People think reporters just wing it. That must be why they think the job is all glamour and no work." She gave me a lopsided smile. I said, "I always research people I'm going to interview. You were photographed, I think by the Washington *Post*, at a party with him ten days ago or so."

"Yes. It's a shock."

The cat stared at the back of Peggy's neck. He jumped from the windowsill to the desk, and from there to the floor. Peggy got up and shut the door to the outer office. The farther door to the hall was open and she didn't want the cat to get out. The cat stalked past the bed, sheared away, and prowled around the wastebasket as if it were some sort of prey.

I said, "I'm sorry. It must be especially hard for you, so soon after moving in, losing one of the few friends you've met here."

"It is. Although maybe if I'd known him longer it'd be worse." She said this calmly, but there was a lot of sadness in her eyes.

I felt extremely sorry for her. At the same time, I was excited and tense, which made it harder to look relaxed and in charge of a chatty interview. The ginger tom crouched, then sprang forward and ran under the desk. I felt like a cat myself, waiting to spring at a mouse.

"Apparently the investigators believe he'd been drinking," I said. "They're reporting ethanol in the blood."

"He did drink. I asked him not to once, because he always drove his own car. Not like a lot of Washingtonians, you know. They seem to think being chauffeured is proof that you're a real success. Anyway, he didn't like it when I asked him not to drink too much, and I didn't want to upset him, so I just dropped the subject."

Didn't want to turn him off, probably. Unfortunately, Peggy was not a person who would be surrounded by men asking her out.

She said, "Washingtonians drink too much, almost all of them."

I went on, "They think there was somebody else in the car with him. Several cars on the bridge stopped when they saw the Porsche crash through the guardrail. A witness said two people swam away."

"I heard that."

"It looks like they both got out safely. The car floated for a while, and they crawled through an open window. Whoever was with him could swim. But he was a very weak swimmer."

"Unless she—unless whoever it was drowned too."

"Well, no. There was a call from a pay phone reporting the accident. Asking for help. Almost certainly the passenger. I guess she hoped the rescue people might save him."

"I guess."

"I shouldn't have said 'she hoped.' The caller whispered and the news reporter said the police didn't know if it was a man or woman."

"Yes, I heard that too."

"She has good reason not to want to be identified."

"Yes. The way it is, she could be anybody."

I was profoundly conscious that this could be the scoop of my career. Carefully, I went on.

"Whoever it was, he or she would be guilty of leaving the scene of an accident."

"And that's a crime," Peggy said, placing her hands together, folding the fingers and squeezing.

"Leaving the scene of a fatal accident. I think it's a felony."

She didn't respond. We sat looking at each other for at least half a minute—a *very* long time in polite social discourse. The ginger tom slipped past me, skirted the blue cushion, jumped to the top of a bookcase, and paced back and forth.

Finally, Peggy said:

"Are you going to report that it was me?"

I hesitated too. From feeling excited, I had gone to feeling sick. Some decision had been made viscerally without my brain being involved. It had to do with how I would feel about this six months from now. What I was about to do was foolish. After all, I had my own career to take care of, didn't I? All right. It was my life. I was free to do what I chose. I was going to be foolish.

I said, "No. You've suffered enough."

"What—?"

I pointed to the cat. "He prowls constantly. He's restless. He won't lie down in that bed."

Peggy wrapped her arms around her chest.

I said, "How else would I have known? MGM went everywhere with you. No wonder you're tired. How many pet stores and animal shelters did you have to go to this morning before you found a tom with exactly that coloring?"

*My husband and I drove the real, original Route 66 one sum-
mer a year after we were married. It was our chance to see
the country, from the Midwest across Kansas, New Mexico,
Arizona, all the way to L.A. There will never be another
highway like it.*

Motel 66

June 11, 1971

About eight miles south of Bloomington-Normal, June finally
convinced Donald to let her drive. At that point they were a
hundred and thirty miles away from Chicago. A hundred and
thirty miles from home. Donald had crossed the middle line too
often, and she was worried about the amount of champagne he
had drunk. The secondhand Packard that was her grandfather's
wedding gift held the road through sheer weight, tacking slowly
like a working sailboat and not much less hefty than a Packard
hearse, but there were giant produce trucks with vertical
wooden pickets holding loads of asparagus coming the other
way, bound to Chicago probably, and June was terrified about
what would happen if Donald steered into one head-on.

Once relieved of driving, David picked a champagne
bottle off the floor of the back seat and swigged some of it.
Donald's brother had put six of the bottles of champagne that
had not been drunk into the car, saying "Celebrate!"

"Do you think you should have all that?" she asked, very
cautiously, not wanting to start off their marriage sounding
like a nag.

"Why, sure, Juney. If I can't drink champagne today, what
day can I ever drink it?"

"Well, that's true."

It was getting late and the sun was low. A noon wedding had been followed by the wedding lunch, then the bouquet-throwing, and finally she had changed into this peach-colored suit and matching little hat, and her new wedding hairstyle. She felt glamorous, but the straight skirt was too tight for comfortable driving. She wondered if she should hike it up, but she would feel brazen to have her thighs exposed. Then she thought, "How silly. We're married." But she still didn't hike it up. Somehow it just didn't seem right.

Her mother had insisted on June and Donald having a good solid snack before they left, and it turned out, much as June hated to admit it, her mother had been right. They would really have been hungry by now otherwise. The woman had also put a package of sandwiches wrapped in wax paper in a bag in the back seat and June had eaten a sandwich while Donald drove. He only seemed to want champagne.

They had passed three or four Motel 66s along Route 66 as they headed south. But they had no connection with each other, Donald said. She said, "Maybe they're a chain, like Howard Johnson's."

But Donald said, "No. Howard Johnson's is restaurants. There aren't any motel chains."

She was sure she'd heard of some, but she didn't want to contradict Donald, because he didn't like being contradicted. And anyway it wasn't important.

Motel 66 Motor Court was nice looking, a dozen separate little cabins painted white with navy blue trim. The cabins were plunked down in a horseshoe shape in the middle of open land. Young trees had been planted between each cabin and the next, but they were saplings and didn't soften the flat, featureless landscape much. June thought that the trees were copper beeches. Donald pulled up to a tiny cabin in the center that had an OFFICE sign in front.

"Do you think we need our marriage license?" June said, as she smoothed her skirt before getting out of the car. She had never checked into a motel before—the idea still made her quite nervous—and she had heard bad things.

"No," Donald said.

"But people say they'll wonder if you're really married, and they check to see if you have luggage—"

By then Donald had entered the door of the office and she followed right away, suddenly feeling alone. As she closed the car door, a little rice blew out. Well, if they don't believe it, she thought, there's the proof.

June heard angry voices, quickly cut off. The office was not more than ten feet by ten feet, with a counter topped with linoleum in the center. The same linoleum covered the floor. The office was spotlessly clean, and in fact a teenage girl with a dustpan and broom was digging dust out of the corner where the two far walls came together.

A cash register sat on a card table against the rear wall. A man sat cranking the handle of an adding machine, holding small sheets of paper in his left hand.

"Welcome to Motel 66," said a pink, plump woman in a pink dress sprigged with blue carnations.

Donald said, "Thanks. We'd like a room."

"How many nights?"

"One."

"That'll be six dollars."

June saw Donald wince, thinking this was more than he had expected to pay. She hoped he wouldn't make a fuss.

The woman seemed to want to gloss over the price too, and talked on breezily. "I'm Bertine, and this is Pete. You're lucky you stopped now. We're full up except for two units."

Pete stood up, saying, "Soon as the sign goes on, people

start coming off the highway."

Donald peeled six ones from his roll of wedding money. Pete was very handsome, June noticed, and he smiled at her, then actually winked. Immediately she told herself loyally that Donald was a good-looking man too.

Donald reached out for the key, a big brass key attached to a piece of wood into which the number three had been burned with a wood-burning tool. June patted her hair, unfamiliar and somewhat uncomfortable in its new style. Rice flew out onto the counter.

"Oh, gee!" she said.

Bertine said, "Why you're just married!"

June blushed. "That's right."

"That's so exciting. Isn't that exciting, Pete?"

"Sure is. Congratulations."

"On your wedding trip?" Bertine said.

"Yes. My uncle has a house near Los Angeles he's lending us for two weeks. And we're seeing the country, the Painted Desert and the Petrified Forest and everything, as we go."

"Well, isn't that the best!"

June ducked her head, still embarrassed because these people would know it was her wedding night.

The cleaning girl tipped up her dustpan to hold the dust and headed for the side door of the office. As she passed behind Pete and Bertine, Pete casually reached his left hand back and patted her bottom. Donald noticed, but June did not, and Bertine was standing to Pete's right and could not have seen.

Donald seized the key and headed for the door. June followed him quickly, afraid somebody might embarrass her with wedding night jokes.

As the screen door closed behind them, June heard Bertine say cheerily, "There. There's another car turning in. We're full."

"Oh, yeah. That's swell, isn't it?"

"It is, Pete."

June stopped to listen. She was interested in people.

"It is *now*," Pete said. "How about in a couple of years? Once the interstate is in. Huh?"

"Maybe it won't be so bad. You know the government. It could be years before they even get started. Prob'ly will be. Decades, maybe."

"I heard they started a section near Bloomington."

"Well, that's there. This is here."

"I told you we should never've bought here. Goddamn President Eisenhower anyhow!"

His hand on the car door, Donald said, "Come on, Juney."

As Donald drove the car over to cabin three, June whispered, "They've been arguing."

Donald said, "Obviously. But it's not our problem."

"Oh, no. Of course not."

"We're on our honeymoon," Donald said. He didn't say anything about Pete patting the cleaning girl.

It was past eight-thirty P.M. now, and the sun was setting.

The cabin was as spotless inside as the office had been. The decor was fake rustic, with red and green plaid linoleum, wood-look wallboard, and a white ceiling with wooden beams. June knew the beams were hollow. Her parents had exactly the same thing in their rec room. But she liked it.

The bathroom didn't quite match. All the fixtures were pink.

June said, "This is so exciting. I know I'm just a silly romantic, but here I am getting married in June and my name is June. It's almost like it's *meant*."

"Most people get married in June."

"Yes. That's true." This was not the answer she'd hoped for. She'd rather he'd said something like, "It feels like it was meant for me, too." Not wanting to be argumentative, she said, "Well, not everybody's name is June."

Donald picked up a bottle of champagne and went to the bathroom to get a glass. "Pete and Bertine must've got a real deal on pink porcelain," he said, coming out. He poured the glass full.

"Uh—should we go get dinner?" June asked. "There's the Moon Shot Restaurant across the street. Just behind the Phillips 66."

"I'm not hungry. Are you?"

"No, I ate a sandwich."

"Then let's go to bed."

Timidly, June picked up her overnight case—white leather, a gift from her aunt Nella—and went into the bathroom. She showered, then splashed on lilac-scented body lotion. A gift from her niece Peggy.

Embarrassed, thrilled, and a little giddy all at the same time, she took the top item from the overnight case. It was a beautiful lace nightgown, with ruffles at the hem and neckline. The girls from the Kresge five-and-dime where June worked had pooled their money and bought it for her. There were some other gifts at the shower that were embarrassing, but June had pretended to be too sophisticated to notice, and if she hadn't blushed so hard, it would have worked. One of the girls confessed that she had actually "done it" with her boyfriend, and the others glanced at one another, thinking, but not saying, that she was a fallen woman.

The nightgown was a lovely orchid color. There had been much laughing at the shower, when two of the girls insisted it was lilac and would "go" with Peggy's lilac scent. Three of them said the color was orchid, and June herself kept saying lavender, and they all giggled. A satin ribbon in darker orchid was threaded through eyelets around the neckline and tied in a bow in front. June wondered briefly if she would look like a candy box, but then thought, no, it was beautiful, and it went well with her dark hair. She slipped it down over her shoulders, wiggled it over her hips, smoothed everything into place with nervous hands and stepped out of the bathroom.

Don lay on the bed, on top of the bedspread, asleep in his clothes.

"Donald?" He didn't stir. "Donald? Here I am."

He still didn't stir, so she touched his shoulder. The glass on the night table was empty. Half of the new bottle of champagne was gone.

"Don?"

Mumbling, he said, "Don' bother—"

June sat down in the only chair in the room, a chair with wooden arms and an upholstered plaid seat and back, and watched Don sleep. After forty-five minutes or so, she tried to wake him again, but he didn't even mumble. She stood and gazed out the window; it was long since dark, and there was no moon.

After a few tears had run down her cheeks, June went to the large suitcase and found some cheese crackers her mother had shoved in at the last minute. She spent another half hour munching them slowly, then tried waking Don again. When that didn't work, she got a glass of water, drank it one swallow at a time, then took dungarees and a sweater from her suitcase, changed out of the lovely nightgown, which she draped carefully across the back of the chair—the extra care was intended to contain her anger—and went out for a walk.

An hour and a half later, June came back to the room. She

let herself in quietly. Don was not there. Feeling guilty, she went into the bathroom and took a shower. When she got out, she looked at herself in the mirror. It was very mysterious, she thought, that you didn't really know who anybody was, not even yourself. "Serves you right, Don," she whispered. Twenty minutes later he turned up.

His eyes were bloodshot. His hair was stiff and stringy, as if he'd been used upside down as a floor mop. She knew he was hung over, but she didn't want to mention it. Instead she said uneasily, "Where have you been?"

He said, "You weren't here." She didn't respond to that.

He said, "I went for a walk."

"Where?"

"Over to the Moon Shot."

"But it closed at ten."

"All I said was I walked over there. I didn't say it was open!"

"Oh."

"And then I walked around a while!"

June and Donald woke up early, even though Donald had a hangover and couldn't open his eyes all the way. They dressed silently, facing away from each other, each not wanting to catch the other's eye. They walked together to the office to return the key.

Finally, Donald said, "Sorry about last night."

Thinking for a few seconds, to try to decide whether she was about to lie or be honest, June finally said, "Me too."

Bertine was alone in the office.

June said, "Well, thanks. It was a—it was a really nice cabin."

"Sure thing," Bertine said, but her eyes were red and puffy and she dragged her feet. It took her several seconds to focus on her job. "Have a happy life," she said. "Come visit again some day."

Donald got behind the wheel of the car. June said soberly, "I guess they've been fighting again."

June 6, 1985

From the back seat, Jennifer, who was seven years old, said, "Why can't we stay at a Holiday Inn? They have a swimming pool."

Donald said, "This is your mother's idea. Not mine. I can think of a lot of better places to be."

June said, "We're having a nostalgia trip."

Don Jr. said, "Well, it's your nostalgia. It's not ours."

They pulled off Interstate 55 onto a deteriorated road that once had been Route 66, running parallel to the interstate. They bumped over potholes so crumbly they must have been unpatched for years. Ahead they saw two concrete islands, four big metal caps over ground pipes, and a shell of the old gas station, two oil bays inside still visible as long narrow depressions with a central hole for the hydraulic lift. There was no sign whatever of the Moon Shot Burgers and Fries. The motel still stood—twelve cabins with beech trees shading them from the summer sun. The cabins were painted white with red trim. The red enamel paint was peeling and the matte white looked chalky and cheap.

June said, "Look, Don, they've changed the name. Now it's the Route 66 Motor Inn."

"This is soooo bogus!" Jennifer said. But she was a nice child, really, and didn't grumble when they stopped the car, even though the place didn't appear to be very prosperous.

Donald said, "A Holiday Inn would be better. Let's go find one."

June said, "No."

Don Jr., usually called Donny, said, "This looks weird."

Donny was thirteen years old. They'd had a fertility problem between Donny and Jennifer, but fortunately nothing permanent. Donny was just starting to make his growth spurt. He hoped by next fall, when he went back to school, he'd discover he'd caught up with the girls in his class, most of whom had put on their growth spurt last year.

He's growing so fast, June thought, studying her gangly child. She could have sworn those pants and the sleeves of the shirt fit when they left Chicago. That was all of six hours ago. Now his wrists stuck out an inch and his ankles an inch and a half. He'd gone up one shoe size a month for the last six months and everybody said feet started to grow first, then the legs. Thank God Donald was a hard-working man.

"Why didn't you go to Florida or something on your honeymoon?" Donny asked.

"Well, partly we had never seen the country. Especially the West. And partly your uncle Mort had a house near Los Angeles that he was going to loan us for two weeks."

"The price was right," Donald said. "Free."

June said, "We had this big old car that your great-grandfather gave us. You'd have laughed at it, Donny."

"Yeah. I wish you'd've kept it."

"Can't keep everything," Donald said.

"You remember your great-grandfather, Donny?"

"Not really. He used to ride me in his wheelbarrow, didn't he?"

Getting out of the car, June said, "We took five days to drive to L.A. We saw the Painted Desert in Arizona, for one thing. And in Amarillo, Texas, we saw a real cattle drive."

Jennifer said, "Big deal."

Donny said, "Why not Las Vegas?"

"We didn't have any money. You kids have been much

more fortunate than we were, you know. Thanks to your dad being a good provider." Well, perhaps he was a little possessive, a little rigid, too, but maybe being solid meant you had to be rigid.

"We always hear that."

"Well, we didn't have any money, but we saw a lot of the wild West."

Jennifer said, "That's okay, Mom. You're entitled to a life."

"We took Route 66 all the way from Chicago to L.A. Did you know there was even a TV show once about Route 66?"

Looking at the potholed road, Jennifer said, "Route 66 isn't here anymore."

"Neither is George Washington," June said. "But we still study him."

All four of them walked into the central cabin, the one with the OFFICE sign above the door. Donald pulled out his credit card. He had three and was proud of them.

June took one look at the woman behind the cash register. "Why, you're still here!" The woman was older, tougher, plumper, and more frayed.

"Do I know you?"

"You're Betty—no, Bertha—"

"Bertine."

"We were here nearly fifteen years ago. June 11, 1971."

"Oh, my God. The newlyweds!"

Donald said, "Come on, Juney. Let's get a key and go."

June said, "Bertine, do you really remember somebody who was here that long ago? I mean, I remember you and your husband, but it was my wedding trip. Everything was important. You must have a dozen new people here every day."

"Mmm, well, now that I see you, I sort of remember." She hesitated. "Actually it wasn't like every other day."

"Why?"

"I might as well tell you. Pete was killed that night."

"Oh!" June felt shock, even though Pete wasn't anything to her, of course. Not really. She could hardly even picture Pete in her mind's eye anymore, which seemed wrong. She ought to remember him. Handsome, she thought, but she somehow confused him in her mind with Robert Redford.

"Was he in an accident?"

"He was beaten to death with a rock. Behind the old Moon Shot restaurant."

"Oh, my God!"

"He never came home that night. I thought he was um— was out, you know, somewhere. They found him when the Moon Shot opened for lunch."

"Who did it?"

"I don't know. We never found out. A drifter, I guess. The cops asked about who was here, in the cabins, you know, so I told them all about everybody. But none of you had anything to do with us. We'd never seen any of you before. They talked with the people who worked for us, but nothing came of it. Just nobody a-tall had a motive. I guess it was just one of those things. He was only twenty-eight."

Since each "cabin" had only one room and one big bed, they took two cabins next to each other, number three and number four. Donald and Donny took number four and June and Jennifer took three.

"Jeez, this is truly bogus!" Jennifer said when they unlocked their door and she saw the tiny room. June thought it didn't seem as clean as she remembered it.

From one door away, Donny said to Jennifer, "Hey! I think it's excellent. How many times do you get to visit the scene of a murder?"

"Get inside, Donny," Donald said.

"But Dad, let's go look at where it happened! She said over by where the restaurant was. Maybe we can find a clue."

"We are *not*," Donald said, veins beginning to stand out on his face, "going to ruin our vacation. And we are not going to say *one more word about murder!*"

June 27, 1999

The sign on Interstate 55 said HISTORIC ROUTE 66! EXIT! HERE!

Just past it, there was a second sign: STAY AT HISTORIC ROUTE 66 MOTEL! ORIGINAL! NOT REBUILT!

And a third sign: SATELLITE BURGERS! JUKE BOXES! MALT SHOP! ONE BLOCK ON RIGHT!

As they came to the exit, a series of six signs in a long row swept past them saying,

!ROUTE 66 AUTO MUSEUM!

SIT IN A REAL 1956 BUICK CENTURY—TWO TONE!

DRIVE AN EDSEL!

Smaller letters under the Edsel offer read: OUR CURATOR MUST ACCOMPANY YOU.

CHEVY BEL AIR—NOT ONE, NOT TWO, THE COMPLETE LINE!

FORD FAIRLANE!

The last sign was shaped like a long hand with a pointing finger and added, ARTIFACTS! NEWSPAPERS! NEIL ARMSTRONG WALKS ON MOON! ORIGINAL FRONT PAGES AND BLOW-UPS! 500 HUBCAPS 500!

It was all so different, with its effort at trying to be the same, June thought. And here we are, back here again, and again the reason is a wedding.

Donny, who was twenty-seven, had dropped out of college

after a year, gone to work for a concrete company, then decided building wooden forms and troweling ready-mix was not a lifetime career for him. He had just graduated from the University of Illinois at Champaign in computer engineering. In his last year he'd met Deborah Henry, who'd been in several classes with him. On June thirtieth they were getting married in St. Louis, where Deborah's family lived.

One more chance, June thought, to drive part of their old, sentimental route.

Jennifer, who was twenty and a junior at Yale, had said, "I'll fly to St. Louis. I did your nostalgia trip once and once was enough."

It wasn't all malt shops and gas-guzzling cars and jukeboxes, June thought. It wasn't romance. It was a lack of options. Her children really believed she was nostalgic. Children were so simple-minded when it came to parents. She was not nostalgic. If she was looking for anything, it was understanding. A search. Who was I then and why?

What a funny, naive little thing I was when we first came here, she thought, uneasily. Brought up with virtually no knowledge of sex and those unreasonable expectations. All twitterpated at the idea of my wedding night. It was such a big deal. Not like these kids.

She remembered Don's anger a couple of years ago when they found condoms in Jennifer's drawer. Fathers can be so unrealistic. And when June tried to tell him condoms were a good thing, and that she had already talked with both children about them, he yelled, "My mother didn't even know the *word* 'condom' and if she had, she would never have uttered it in my presence."

"I'm sure, dear," June had said mildly.

They pulled into the Motel 66 driveway.

"Dad, can I take the car over to that museum shop? They

might have moon landing stuff. Memorabilia."

"Absolutely not. If you want the car, I'll go with you."

Donny, who'd been through this before, said indulgently, "Yeah, Dad. I know. What's yours is yours." To June he said, "Mom, it's only two blocks. I'll walk fast over there and see what they've got. Five minutes."

"Just three minutes," Donald said. "We need to find a place to eat."

Historic Motel 66 was surrounded by recently mowed bright green grass. Huge beech trees shaded the cabins, except for a gap down toward the end, where a cabin was missing and half a tree remained next to the space, a split trunk leaning eastward. Lightning, June thought.

The bright white and blue paint looked new. The colors struck a chord in June's memory, but she couldn't quite be sure.

She and Donald entered the office. The old cash register was back. The walls were covered with black and white blow-ups of Motel 66, each meticulously dated, and a professionally produced sign above them read, THE HISTORY OF MOTEL 66!

Behind the counter stood a trim white-haired woman in a black power suit over a sapphire blue silk shirt.

June said, "Oh! Isn't Bertha, uh, Ber—um, isn't she here anymore?"

"I'm Bertine."

"Bertine! I wouldn't have known you!"

Bertine smiled. "I figured if I was gonna spruce up the place I'd spruce up myself too. I kind of remember you, honey, but not quite."

"We're what you called the newlyweds. From 1971. June 11, 1971."

"Oh." Bertine's eyes clouded for a few seconds. "I have to say, I've brought the place along a bit since then. Pete would still recognize it, though."

"It looks great!"

"Well, I'm doing okay. This isn't a way to get rich. But I make decent money. Now. It was hard going for a while."

Donald pulled out his credit cards. "Let me get the keys," he said. "We've gotta go eat."

Bertine said, "See, I have the old cash register, but I hardly know how to take cash anymore. My accountant says never take cash and surely never let any of the help take cash." She laughed. "There's a fragment of Route 66 from Oklahoma City to Vinita, Oklahoma, if you're touring. And a piece of historic 66 in Albuquerque."

June said, "We're not going to L.A. this time. Just St. Louis."

She thought about Uncle Mort, who had loaned them his house. Uncle Mort had run off with a girl he met at his health club, where he was working out because his doctor told him to. The girl was a cardio-fitness trainer, but June's mother would still have called her a flibbertigibbet, if June's mother were still alive.

June walked over to the photo blow-ups. One showed the construction of the cabins and was dated March 27, 1969. One showed a line of late-sixties cars on the curved driveway near the motel office.

Bertine walked over to the photos behind her. June had stopped in front of a big photo of Bertine and Pete, holding hands under a MOTEL 66 sign at the door of the brand new office.

Donald said, "Come on, Juney. I'm hungry."

"Poor Pete," Bertine said, but June's back was rigid and she didn't turn around.

Donny came bursting in, shouting, "I got a reproduction 1969 *New York Times* moon landing page. Debbie's gonna think it's real fun." When he entered, Bertine caught sight of him and she froze, staring.

Donny came to a stop next to the photo of Pete, age probably twenty-seven.

For a second, Bertine looked back and forth between the photo and Donny.

Bertine tried to ask June something, but the words caught in her throat. It was something like "no motive." June made a small whimpering sound. Then she turned in fear to Donald.

When she saw the expression on his face, she started to scream.